TURN THE JOKER AROUND

TURN THE JOKER AROUND

By Alice Zogg

Aventine Press

This book is a work of fiction.

First Edition

Published by Aventine Press
1023 4th Ave #204
San Diego CA, 92101
www.aventinepress.com

ISBN: 1-59330-188-X

Library of Congress Cataloging-in-Publication Data
2004109382

Printed in the United States of America

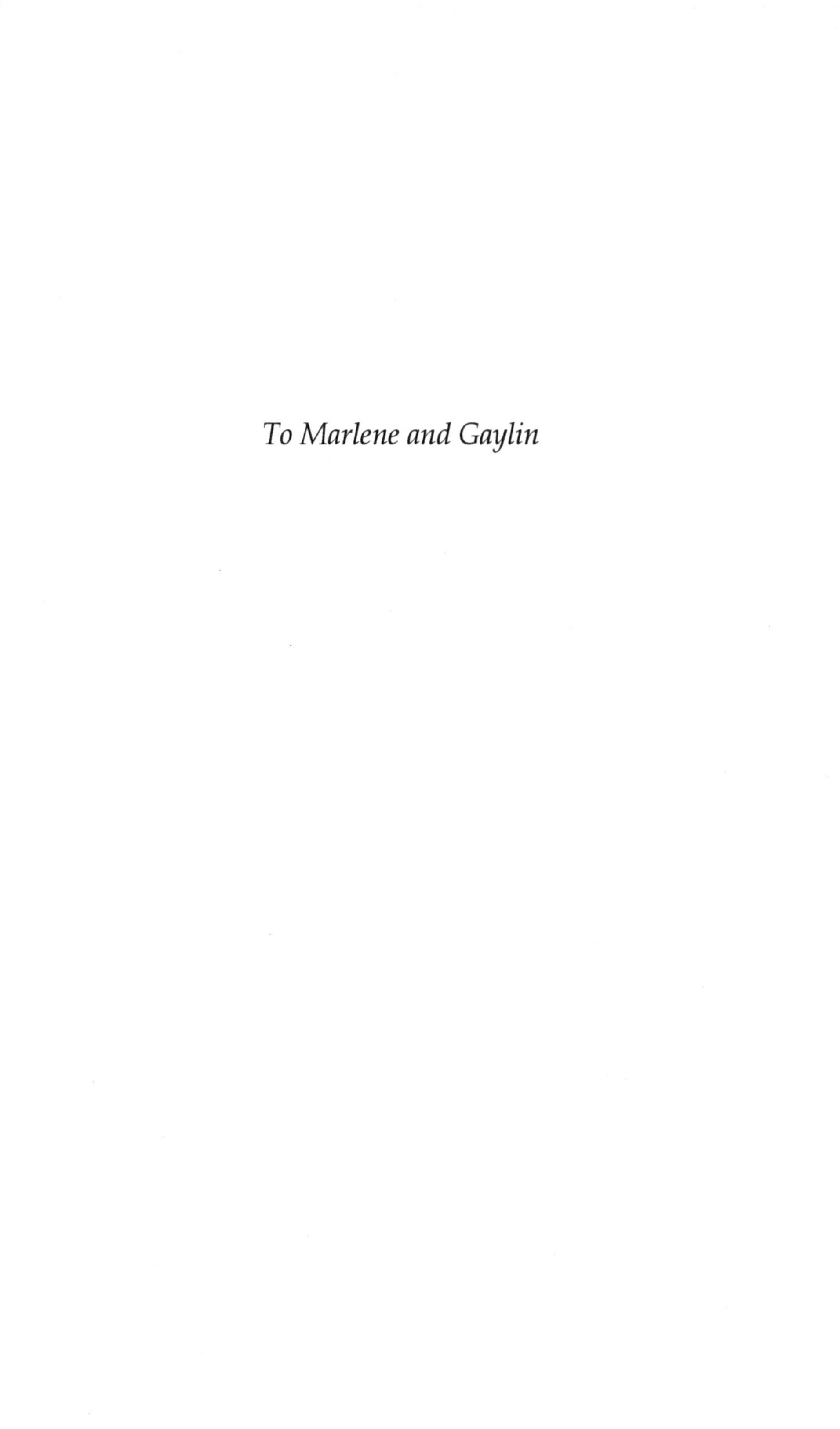

To Marlene and Gaylin

CREDITS:

Once more my gratitude goes to Editor Charles Watry for his skillful manuscript evaluation and critique. Credit is due to my good friends, Marlene and Gaylin Schultz, for their contribution of local color on Santa Catalina Island in general, and the mechanism of golf carts in particular. Thanks are in order to Joan Joe, for answering my numerous medical questions. My son-in-law Sam's expert input on scuba diving is greatly appreciated. Thank you, Sam. My friend, Pat Yankosky, came to the rescue again; this time she enlightened me about the mechanics of creating bronze sculptures and the proper name of sculpting tools. Thanks to my daughter, Franziska, for her tedious job of proofreading. I value her time consuming task.

CAST OF CHARACTERS:

R. A. Huber Private detective and narrator of this story

Peter Huber R. A. Huber's husband; an amateur writer

Lillian (Lillie) Robertson Executive of pharmaceutical company in Boston

Mildred (Millie) Faracelli Lillian's twin sister; wealthy, eccentric; has a flair for discovering new and upcoming talents

Tony Faracelli Mildred's stepson; an unemployed pilot

Lisa Faracelli Tony's pregnant wife

Gina Faracelli Mildred's stepdaughter; a model

Guido Faracelli Mildred's stepson; entrepreneur; seems to have a bit of a gambling problem

Jesse Limburg Troubled juvenile delinquent; recently developed a passion for scuba diving

Michael Albertis Mildred's newest discovery; an artist

Beatrix Primrose Very capable housekeeper

Dr. Charles Timble Gina's fiancé; G.P. on the island; would prefer to spend his time doing research, but is lacking funds

Pamela Norris Art exhibits coordinator; takes herself very seriously

Julia Jacobs Teenage neighbor of the Faracelli household; seems wise beyond her years.

Bruce Dillon Jesse's tutor; has the patience of a saint

Detective Ron Barker Police Officer of the Los Angeles County Sheriff Homicide Squad; called to case by Avalon's Deputy Sheriff

Chapter 1

◇◇◇◇◇◇◇◇◇◇◇◇◇◇◇◇◇

I had just settled into my chair when the phone rang.

"R.A. Huber," I said.

"This is Lillie. Just making sure you're there. I'm in a cab on my way to your office. See you in a few minutes!"

I was trying to remember when I had last seen Lillian Robertson. I had just come to the conclusion that it must have been at the twins' 50th birthday party, ten years ago, when the door was abruptly flung open and she came toward me with outstretched arms.

She said, "Reg, it sure is good to see you!"

I could not recall the last time anybody had called me 'Reg'! She looked exactly the way I had remembered her, tall and willowy. Her short, stylish ash blond hair enhanced her intelligent gray eyes, straight nose, and generous mouth. If she had aged in the last ten years, it certainly was not noticeable to my eyes.

Embracing her, I exclaimed, "Lillie, you haven't changed a bit. You look as stunning and sophisticated as ever!"

She replied, "You don't look half bad yourself!" And she added, "I noticed the impressive sign on the door, *R. A. Huber, Private Detective.*"

"Has a nice ring to it, doesn't it," I said.

I offered her coffee, and cups in hand, we settled across from each other at my oak desk. Lillie looked around my one-person office, amused, it seemed.

I said, "What?"

She laughed and answered, "This is exactly the way I'd picture an office of yours: neat, no frills, and strictly functional!"

Then her eyes rested on my Staunton Rosewood chess set at one corner of the desk, and she commented, "I hope you didn't set this up for us. I don't think I'm in the mood for playing."

I said, "Oh no. I always have it set up. It is sort of my trademark. Sometimes I play by myself."

Then I said, "After your call, I was thinking back to our time at the *Internat*."

She said, "We sure raised hell in that school. It seems that was a lifetime ago!"

"Yes. Remember, we called ourselves the 'Three Musketeers': Lillie, Millie and Reg!"

Lillie chuckled and said, "We had a lot of fun together. Remember playing pranks and tricks on the nuns and getting ourselves into endless trouble? Some of the punishments given to us, when we got caught, bordered on bizarre!"

I replied, "Like the time the *Révérende Mère* made us go to the kitchen and help the domestics peel about 100 potatoes. Little did the good nun realize that we much preferred to chat with the kitchen staff than sit in silence concentrating on our homework in the study hall."

Lillie asked, "What was it that the *Révérende Mère* always quoted, just before she announced the punishment?"

I said, " *'Tournons le farceur':* Let's turn the joker around."

"That's it." And she added, "I wonder what Mother Superior would say now, if she could see us. You, a successful private eye; Millie, a well-known sculptress; and myself, head of a major pharmaceutical company!"

I replied, "I'm sure she and most of the other nuns are all dead and gone by now. They seemed old then. But of course at that time, everyone over 30 seemed ancient to us."

Then I said, "Enough of the past. How are you doing now? I take it your company is prospering under your guidance?"

Lillie smiled and said, "Yes. It is doing quite well. When Sal died, and stated in his will that I was to be the executive of the company, I was terrified. At the time I felt I was in this way over my head. As you know, that was three years ago. I pulled myself together, surrounded myself with knowledgeable, trustworthy people, and got educated about the business. Now, I feel that I know what I'm doing, and what's more, I truly enjoy it."

I said, "Attagirl!"

After a pause I said, "Now Lillie, I've a feeling you did not come all the way from Boston to reminisce about the past with me. What brings you here today?"

She said, "You are right. There is a problem, and I want to hire you. I'm worried about Millie."

"What's the matter with Millie? Is she sick?"

"Oh no. Nothing to do with her health."

"So?"

"Well, Reg, I can't put my finger on it. I have bad vibes. I just know there is something terribly wrong in Millie's household. Something is going on and I can't figure out from what direction."

"Can you explain yourself a little better?"

She sighed, and then said, "Have you kept in contact with Millie?"

"Not much. We exchange Christmas cards and every so often I get a postcard when she travels. I have noticed that her name has changed a few times, but when I heard from her last, she went by the name of Faracelli again."

Lillie said, "Yes, she switched back to Faracelli after her last marriage ended."

Then she said, "OK. I think I'd better fill you in on all her marriages and bring you up to date about her life at present. I'm sure you know about her first and second husbands, but I'll refresh your memory, just in case.

"Millie married Henry Sebastian when she was very young. She was only in her first year of college at the time.

Henry was quite a bit older than her and owned his own business. I believe it was manufacturing plastics. Millie finished her education while married to Henry."

I said, "I was invited to the wedding but could not attend. I was still living in Switzerland at the time, and in those days you did not fly to another continent on such occasions, unless it was a close relative who was getting married."

Lillie continued, "Henry died of a heart attack when only in his early forties. As a result, Millie was a widow at age 25. She was an art major and already starting to show talent in the field. I'm sure you remember husband number two, architect Anthony Faracelli. He was the love of her life. I always felt that Anthony and Millie had been made for each other. It was devastatingly tragic when, as you know, Anthony died in a car crash."

I interrupted, "There were children. Three, I believe?"

She answered, "Yes, Anthony brought three children into the marriage."

"You mean none of the children were Millie's? I thought at least the youngest was hers?"

"No. Millie never had children of her own, but she sure was, and still is, a great mother to those kids. Anthony's car accident happened when all the children were still in elementary school."

I said, "Peter and I were present at Millie's wedding to Anthony. I remember they seemed very much in love. I also remember that you, Lillie, were on cloud nine yourself, having just gotten engaged to Sal!"

She replied, "Oh, I remember it well!"

I then asked, "Bringing three children into a marriage, Anthony was either a widower or else his ex must have been real bad news. I never asked Millie. I didn't want to pry."

Lillie said, "He was a widower. His first wife died giving birth to Guido, the youngest son."

"Oh, how sad," I said.

She continued, "Millie was 30 when she married Anthony and had an instant family. The children --Tony, Gina and Guido -- were age six, four and two at that time. Six years later, Millie was a widow for the second time. She was thrown into single parenthood instantaneously and, in my opinion, did a wonderful job. Money was no problem. She was able to devote all her time to her family and pursue her art as well. I don't think she as much as looked at any man twice in the next ten years."

I said, "I'm glad you refreshed my memory about her first two husbands. Even though I had known them, I didn't have all the facts straight, especially where the children were concerned." And I added, "What comes next will definitely be news to me. So please continue."

Lillie laughed and said, "It sounds a little like a soap opera already, but hang on, it will get even more so!"

Then she said, "Now, where was I? Oh yes, getting to husband number three. I must say, in the years that she was rearing the children, she was not totally idle in other respects. As I said, she kept up her art, and by the time the last kid entered college, she had already made a name for herself in those circles. I personally always liked her charcoal drawings best, but for many years she concentrated on making sculptures."

She grinned at me and said, "By the way, have you seen any of her sculptures?"

I nodded and replied, "Yes. I visited one of her exhibits, and some of the figures were in somewhat risqué positions! I think, though, that her greatest talent shows itself in the way she captures facial expressions."

Lillie continued, "Millie is not only interested in her own type of art but enjoys and is knowledgeable about all forms of the arts. She has developed a knack for discovering new artistic talents in all avenues of the field. She sponsors art exhibits, theater plays, talent shows, poetry clubs, you name it. If she finds a project or person she thinks worthwhile having to do with fine or performing arts, she'll throw money into it."

I inquired, "I take it she has a lot of money to throw?"

"Yes. Millie is wealthy. She inherited money from our parents, to begin with. Then Henry left her quite a fortune. Anthony Faracelli had advised her to invest most of her money in real estate rather than buy stocks. I guess that was natural, coming from an architect. Consequently, when a lot of people lost tons of money in the recent stock slump, it did not affect her. On the contrary, real estate is booming, and her money multiplies all on its own. She could live off her artwork, if she chose, but she actually has sold very little of it. She prefers to donate the pieces to museums, or give them as presents."

Lillie continued, "Husband number three, Richard Rumpland, came on the scene when Millie was 46. He is an opera singer, a tenor, to be exact. Millie 'discovered' and promoted him. She had some influence in the world of stage and opera. He turned out to be very talented indeed. He is one of the most famous tenors at the moment."

I interrupted, saying, "I've never heard of a Richard Rumpland."

Lillie chuckled and said, "Of course you haven't. He changed his name. Calls himself Rico Ramono now."

I exclaimed, "*The* Rico Ramono?"

"The same!"

"Wow! Millie surely has an eye for talent!" Then I asked, "The marriage did not work out?"

She replied, "They were only married two years. He started to show a sexual preference in men. They had an amiable divorce, he thanked Millie kindly for all she'd done for him, and took a plane to Venice, Italy, where I think he still lives 'happily ever after.'"

Lillie paused, and then said, "She married husband number four, Jason Limburg, about ten years ago."

I said, "I saw you and Millie at your combined 50th birthday party, but I don't recall her bringing any husband along."

"No. He was not at the party, but Millie married him a couple of months later."

Lillie went on, "Jason is, or I should say was, a playwright. Yes, Reg, you guessed it, another one of Millie's discoveries. Jason was a very talented poet and playwright. Millie helped him along, introduced him to the right people who in turn opened the right doors for him. Millie helped finance some of his plays along the way. He became a success."

"Something tells me this marriage was not a success, though?"

"Actually, the marriage itself would have worked out. They seemed relatively happy for about five years. The problem was, Jason could not handle his fame and all the pressures it brought with it. He turned to alcohol, and then one day he just left town. No one seems to know where he is, or how he is."

I asked, "How was Millie taking this?"

Lillie answered, "Oh, Millie was OK. You know her: She's always 'OK'. It caused some problems with the boy, though."

"You mean there is a child?"

"Yes. His name is Jesse. Jason Limburg has a son from a former marriage."

"This Jesse did not live with Millie and Jason, right?"

"Wrong. Jesse did live with them. As a matter of fact, he still lives with Millie now."

"Jesus! Another kid dropped off as a wedding present. I can't believe it!"

And I asked, "Where is Jesse's mother? Has she vanished too?"

Lillie shook her head sadly and said, "She abandoned both Jesse and his father when the boy was only two years old. Jason later found out that she had died a few years later of a drug overdose."

"How very tragic," I said.

"It sure is. Jason could not bring the boy up by himself. He was struggling financially and emotionally after his wife had left him. Jason's parents took care of their grandson for a few years. They had Jason late in life and were already old by then. The grandmother passed away when Jesse was seven, and the grandfather was forced to live in a convalescent home soon after that. Millie entered their lives about then. As you put it, Jesse came as a wedding gift."

I said, "OK, so Millie was 50 and was taking on a seven-year-old stepson. Correct?"

"Correct."

"That sounds a little nutty to me, but I can imagine Millie made the best of it and gave him a good home."

"You've got that right. Jesse was a bit of a problem child even back then, which was understandable given the circumstances. Millie never was a big disciplinarian, but as far as I know, she took him in as one of her own, just like she had done previously with the Faracelli children."

I said, "So when Jesse's father disappeared, the boy become even more of a problem child?"

"Yes."

"How old was the boy when his father left?"

"About twelve."

I said, "That's a crucial age in a boy's development. The timing of his father's skipping town couldn't have been much worse. How old is Jason, by the way?"

"I think he is five years younger than Millie."

I did some arithmetic and said, "He was 45 when he married Millie, his son was seven at the time, and so he is not exactly the youngest of fathers either."

Then I said, "You mentioned that the boy still lives with Millie now. According to my calculations, he is seventeen and should be in his senior high school year by now."

Lillie said, "I hope he makes it into his senior year, come September. Millie hired a tutor for the summer to get him caught up with his junior year studies. Let me explain. As I said, after his father left, there were behavior problems. As he progressed into his teens, his conduct got worse. Being a teenager nowadays isn't easy, even in the best of circumstances, let alone for someone in his shoes."

I interrupted, saying, "Being a teenager was never easy. Not now, not at any time!"

She said, "Yes, you are right. It was never easy."

She continued, "Jesse got into trouble with the law. He was dealing drugs and got arrested. It was his first offense, and the judge ordered him to do community service, which he did. After he had served his required hours, Millie agreed to keep him under strict supervision, and so he was released into her care. Jesse's grades were horrible this year to begin with, and after court appearances and his service to the community, he had missed too much schooling to catch up. The tutor seems to think he can get Jesse ready for his last high school year, come fall."

"How is he behaving now?"

"He is sulky and resentful, but as far as I know, he seems to have shaped up concerning the drugs."

There was a pause. Then I commented, "You have brought me up to date about Millie's life, but you have not enlightened me yet as to what concerns you about Millie. I have the feeling that whatever is worrying you has nothing to do with her stepson's problems."

Lillie said, "I'm getting there. Just bear with me."

"Sorry, I'm not trying to rush you," I said.

"I don't know if you're aware that Millie spends most of her summers on Catalina Island now."

"No. That is news to me."

"She has a residence in Avalon on Santa Catalina Island. She goes there whenever she feels like it during the entire year, but in the summers she moves her whole household to the island. I've just been there for a seven-day visit, and I feel that there is something very wrong going on. As I said earlier, I can't even figure out who or what is making me so uneasy. I just know that there is some evil undercurrent present in that house. If I had time, I might have stayed a few days longer. I'm sure that eventually I could figure out what's going on, but I simply have to get home to Boston. I can't miss an important board meeting tomorrow. I'm flying out of here at 4:00 this afternoon."

She looked at me pleadingly and said, "I've had a couple of sleepless nights trying to decide what to do. I woke up this morning and thought of you. I want to hire you. I hope you're not too busy with other cases, since I want you to hop on a boat to Catalina and stay with Millie for as long as it takes to figure things out."

I replied, "I'm more or less free to do so at the moment. I need more information, however, before I can agree to anything. Tell me about all the people in the household. Who lives there besides Millie?"

She said, "Her stepson, Jesse; Michael Albertis, her newest discovery; Beatrix Primrose, the housekeeper. That is all for the actual live-ins, but there are a lot of comings and goings of visitors all summer long. The Faracelli children were all visiting while I was there. Tony and his wife, Lisa, stayed for three days. Gina seems to be spending a lot of her summer on Catalina this year. I understand her fiancé, a doctor, has his practice on the island. Guido dropped by for the weekend."

I said, "I hope she has a lot of guest bedrooms to accommodate all these extra people."

Lillie smiled and said, "You haven't changed, Reg. Practical as ever! Yes, Millie's house is big and has plenty of guest rooms."

Then I inquired, "Who is this newest discovery of Millie's, Michael Albertis?"

"Michael is a painter and Millie's boyfriend."

I raised an eyebrow and said, "Still going strong at 60, Millie is?"

Lillie burst out laughing and said, "I guess so. At first Millie's interest was strictly in his art, but then it evolved into something more, and he moved in. I've seen some of his work, and he is very talented."

I said, "He would have to be, to qualify as Millie's new protégé!" And I added, "How old is Michael?"

"44."

"So, Lillie, what you really want me to do is check out this Michael Albertis. Do a background check on him, et cetera."

"No. Actually, I've already done that."

"I'm impressed. What did you find out?"

"He has no criminal record. Not even a traffic ticket. He was married once, when very young, and got divorced soon afterwards. No children..."

I interrupted, "Well, thank God for that!"

Lillie continued, "His mother is alive and lives in the Southern California area. Other than that, there are no close relatives. He seems to have led a blameless life so far. When Millie discovered him, he was a struggling artist. Millie is seeing to it that things might change for the better. She is sponsoring an exhibit of his paintings, as we speak."

I said, "So if your feelings of bad vibes have nothing to do with Michael, what exactly do you have in mind?"

"Reg, haven't I already told you more than once, I don't know. I want you to find out for me."

I said, "You must have some kind of an inkling. Bad vibes usually have some foundation. Does the Faracelli bunch resent Michael, for instance? How do they get along with Millie? Do you think that Millie is in danger? Do you think somebody else is in danger? Give me something, Lillie, I beg you!"

Lillie looked at me intently and then said, "OK. I do have something, but it's not much. I don't think any of the kids -- I probably shouldn't call them kids, they're all adults now except for Jesse --are pleased to have Michael Albertis on board. I think they are worried that Millie might marry again. They've all been sponging off Millie for years. She lets them, so that is not a problem. While on my visit, I learned that Millie fell down her stairs at the beginning of May. She wasn't badly injured, just had a slight concussion and sprained her ankle. Then someone hinted that she might have been pushed. That fall, and my feelings of ill will in that household, is what started me worrying."

I said, "Did you ask Millie about her fall down the stairs?"

"Yes, of course."

"What was her explanation?"

"Millie said that sometimes when she can't sleep, she gets up during the night and goes down to the kitchen for something to drink. She said that apparently she just lost her footing and fell. She does not think she was pushed."

"Do you believe her?"

"Well, yes. She wouldn't lie to me on purpose. But you know how vague Millie is."

I said, "Yes, Millie was always vague and seemed somewhere in a world of her own. Is she still that way?"

"Now more so than ever," Lillie replied.

"Who told you that she might have been pushed?"

Lillie thought about this for a minute, then said, "I can't recall who told me. Does it matter?"

"Probably not."

"Do you think I'm crazy to worry?"

"Not at all." And I asked, "Had Michael already moved in when Millie fell down the stairs?"

"Oh no. It happened at Millie's winter residence, before she moved to Catalina for the summer. Michael just started living with Millie in June."

"Does Millie know of your plan to hire me?"

"Of course not. She wouldn't approve."

"What do you suggest I tell her when showing up at her door?"

"I've got it all figured out. I'll tell her I ran into you today and that you're overworked and in desperate need of a vacation. She'll invite you to come spend some relaxing time with her on Catalina."

"You would deceive your twin sister?"

"Yes, I certainly would."

"OK, Lillie, you're on. I can't make any promises. I might not find anything wrong in Millie's household."

"Nothing would please me better than getting a confirmation that all is well!"

I looked at my watch and exclaimed, "It's past noon already. Can you do lunch?"

"No. I've got to run. I have a plane to catch."

She reached inside her purse, pulled a check out and handed it to me. She jumped to her feet, hurried to the door, then turned back towards me and, blowing a kiss in my direction, said, "Thanks, Reg, you're a doll!"

Chapter 2

◇◇◇◇◇◇◇◇◇◇◇◇◇◇◇◇◇

Driving home to Merida from my office in Pasadena that day in July, I reflected on the visit I had from my friend, and I found myself dwelling in the past.

Lillie, Millie, and I had been inseparable buddies while attending a boarding school in Fribourg, the French-speaking part of Switzerland. That seemed centuries ago. The three of us kept in touch over the years but seldom actually got together.

My thoughts coming back to the present, I could not erase the picture of Lillie's worried face from my mind.

Dinner over with that evening, settled into our respective recliners, I surveyed my husband, Peter. His curly hair had started to gray years ago and was now pure white. The prominent eyebrows above his sensitive hazel eyes, as well as the mustache, remained brown. He continued to be slim and trim for a man in his sixties.

Peter suddenly looked up from his book and said, "What's the matter with my face?"

I smiled, and replied, "Not a thing! We've grown old together, but you're still my hero!"

Then I asked, "How do you feel about being left alone while I stay on Santa Catalina Island for a while?"

He replied, "What? You'd go to Catalina without me? Not fair!"

"Sorry, Hon. I know you love the island, but I might have to go there on a job."

"Oh?"

"Remember my friends the twins, Lillie and Millie? We went to their elaborate birthday party about ten years ago."

Peter said, "Yes, I do. Didn't we also go to the wedding of one of them a long time ago?"

"Yes. To Millie's wedding when she married Anthony Faracelli. Anyhow, Lillie came to my office today."

"Is she the ditsy one or the matter-of-fact one? I don't remember which is which. All I recall is that they seemed to be surprisingly different for twins."

I replied, "Yes. Even though they resemble each other in looks slightly, they are very different in character. Don't forget, they are not identical twins. I would not call Millie 'ditsy', however. She is vague, and gives the impression of being in another world, but she is intelligent. I've always had the feeling that Millie knows exactly what goes on around her. To answer your question, Lillie is the matter-of-fact one."

Peter asked, "She's the one that lives on the East Coast, correct?"

"Yes. She lives in Boston."

"Didn't her husband pass away recently?"

"I'm surprised at your good memory, Peter! Yes, Sal Robertson died three years ago. We received a notice but could not fly to Boston to attend his funeral. Remember, we had already made plans for a trip to Canada at the time. Lillie is the main executive of Sal's pharmaceutical company now and apparently enjoys the job."

Then Peter said, "Millie is the artist, right?"

I replied, "Yes. Millie is a talented artist. She has done oil paintings, charcoal drawings, caricatures, but her specialty is sculptures."

"Oh, I remember now. You pointed out some sculptures of hers once, when we visited an art exhibition. Some of her work was interesting, to say the least." And he winked at me.

He continued, "I seem to recall that she lives in our general area?"

"Her main residence is in South Pasadena. I've been there occasionally," I said.

Then he asked, "So, what has all that got to do with your going to Catalina by yourself?"

I said, "It's a long story," and I proceeded to tell him all I had learned from Lillian.

After hearing me out, Peter commented, "Millie's life sounds like a melodrama to me."

"Yes, but knowing Millie, I can easily picture it."

"Does her sister think there might be something wrong with the lover, I believe you said Michael is his name?"

"No, I don't think so."

"Why did she have his background checked, then?"

"I have the feeling she did that as a matter of course. Don't forget, Millie is very rich."

Peter said, "Ah, yes, being wealthy always seems to complicate matters."

Then he said, "Do you think Lillie suspects that one of the stepchildren pushed her sister down the stairs?"

I replied, "I don't know. If Millie was really pushed, I'll have to find out who was present in her house at the time. But she might just have fallen by losing her footing, like she claims."

Peter asked, "How old are those kids anyhow? I guess they'd be in their thirties by now?"

"Give me a second, I need to do some math. When Anthony died, Millie was 36 and the kids were twelve, ten and eight. Millie is my age, so she is 60 now. The difference is 24 years. So that makes Tony 36, Gina 34 and Guido 32. Jesse, the child left in her care from her last marriage, is 17."

Peter said, "Except for Jesse, the rest seem way too old to be sponging off their mother."

I said, "I agree."

Peter paused for a minute and then went on, "I'm sure you thought about all this already. But if Millie said she fell down the stairs by accident -- and vague or not, the woman ought to know if she was pushed or fell -- I don't understand her sister's bad feelings about the household."

I said, "Lillie is a very down-to-earth person. If she feels there is something wrong going on, I trust her judgment. It might have nothing to do with Millie's safety. Hopefully, the bad vibes that Lillie sensed are not putting anyone in danger and are just a matter of spite and ill will. I aim to find out from what direction these vibes are coming from."

Peter said, "Millie agrees with her sister to hire you?"

I answered, "She does not know that Lillie wants me to look into this matter. Lillie will tell her sister that I am in need of a vacation and talk her into inviting me to Catalina."

"Well, have a good time!"

"The canned foods in the pantry, as well as the dinners in the freezer, should hold you over for a while."

Nodding, Peter said, "And there is always *'Chez Tante Jeanne's'* cuisine!"

I said, "Yes, of course. There is always good old Aunt Jeanne."

"When are you leaving?"

"As soon as I get an invitation," I said.

Chapter 3

◇◇◇◇◇◇◇◇◇◇◇◇◇◇◇◇◇

The formal invitation arrived in the mail a few days later. I was cordially invited to spend some time at the Faracelli summer residence on Santa Catalina Island. I was to let them know on which day and by what boat I would arrive. Someone would come pick me up at the harbor. The letter was signed "Mildred Faracelli." A Catalina Express boat schedule was enclosed.

I made a boat reservation, called Millie to accept her kind offer, made another phone call to Boston to let Lillie know that her plan had worked, and packed my suitcase.

Next day, a Wednesday, Peter drove me down to Long Beach, so I did not have to leave my car in the dock's parking lot. The boat was scheduled to leave at 9:30AM, but passengers were required to be there an hour before departure. Allowing for rush-hour traffic, we left our home at 6:30.

On our drive there, I said, "Thanks for getting up at the crack of dawn for my sake."

Peter replied, "That's what husbands are for!"

"Well, I appreciate it. I'm taking you away from writing your new book. By the time you get back to Merida, it will be afternoon."

Peter said, "That's OK. I'm still in the research stage, anyhow."

As we were driving along on the Long Beach freeway, Peter fell silent, obviously engrossed in the heavy truck traffic, that particular route being the main access for trucks to and from both the Los Angeles and Long Beach harbors.

Once we were close to our destination, Peter asked, "Did you pack your gun?"

"Yes. It was an afterthought. I threw it in the top of my suitcase. Hopefully I won't need it."

"They might search your bags before boarding the Catalina Express. In which case you'll have a lot of explaining to do!"

I said, "Yes. I thought of that. After September 11th, it is highly possible that everyone's luggage will be searched. I have the gun permit in my purse, of course, but they might still give me a hard time. They can call Lillie in Boston to verify that I'm on my way to a job. Maybe it's a good thing we have to be there an hour early. If they don't let me take the gun on board, not even tucked away in a suitcase, I guess you'll have to take it back home with you."

Peter asked, "I assume the gun isn't loaded?"

I said, "Of course not. I packed the ammunition separately."

"Well, let's hope your suitcase passes inspection."

After parking the car and picking up the reserved ticket at the counter, we still had over an hour to kill before I could get in line to board. We made ourselves comfortable on a bench in the waiting area.

Peter turned to me and said, "How are you planning to look into this matter, since you're officially supposed to be on vacation? I mean, you can't possibly question all the members of the household, without arousing their suspicions!"

I answered, "Good point. I guess I'll just have to play it by ear. Hopefully I can get information out of them in the course of conversations. They will probably think of me as a nosy old lady. I'm optimistic that if they find me a sympathetic listener, they will open up. People usually like to talk about themselves."

"True."

"And if I am found out, and I have to 'come out of the closet', so to speak, it might actually make my job easier."

"How so?"

"Think about it, Peter. If they know I'm a detective and my purpose for being there is to look into things that aren't kosher, they'll want to cooperate to show they have nothing to hide."

"Yes. I see what you mean now."

Folks were starting to form a line for boarding. I made my way to the end of the queue. Peter stayed with me until we reached the gate. We kissed good-bye and I promised to call in a few days. No one searched my suitcase. As I walked down the ramp to board, I turned my head and saw Peter still standing at the gate. He looked relieved, and I made a thumbs-up gesture in his direction.

I found a window seat inside the Catalina Express. As the boat headed towards the open sea, I looked out at the famous Queen Mary. The elegant ship remains permanently docked in the Long Beach harbor. The city purchased it in 1967 and after three years of renovation opened it as a sightseeing attraction to the general public. The Queen Mary has a glorious and romantic past. The ship was built in Scotland and embarked on its maiden voyage in 1936 from Southampton to New York in record time of only five days. During World War II, it was given the name "Grey Ghost" when it was camouflage-painted and used for military transport. Now, at its repose in the Long Beach harbor, the ship boasts restaurants, shops, tours, entertainment, banquet facilities and a hotel with over 300 staterooms and suites. It contains beautiful wall murals and carvings made of precious woods and an elegant ballroom designed to welcome royalty.

The one-hour trip to Avalon, the capital of Catalina, was relatively smooth on that gorgeous, sunny day in mid July. As the boat approached the island, I was in awe of the picturesque scene. I had been to Avalon a few times before, and with each visit felt a sense of marvel at this quaint, remote little town. One of the first sights that came into view was the Catalina Casino Building with its rounded façade and ornate pillars supporting the balcony. Rows of boats were anchored in the small harbor. Predominantly white and light-colored homes in a variety of styles adorned the surrounding hills. Despite my mission, I felt elated to have come to Avalon.

Chapter 4

◇◇◇◇◇◇◇◇◇◇◇◇◇◇◇◇◇◇

Disembarking the boat, I stood at the quay, admiring the scenery around me. A teenager, dressed in a pair of baggy, khaki shorts that reached way below his knees and a white sleeveless tee shirt, approached me. His head was shaved, numerous studs adorned both his ears, and he was sporting rather large tattoos on his upper arms. Despite the getup and his brusque manner, there was something slightly forlorn about him.

He said, "Mrs. Huber?"

I smiled and said, "Yes."

"I'm Jesse. I'm here to pick you up." And grabbing my suitcase, he grumbled, "Let's go."

I followed him in the direction of the town. We got to an area where golf carts were neatly parked in a row. Cars were a rarity on the island; golf carts were the preferred mode of transportation. The fact that they were allowed to operate on public streets was due to the small area and crowded street conditions. The number of full-sized automobiles was strictly controlled. People were put on a waiting list for several years before permitted to bring a car to Avalon. Jesse led me to a golf cart with a green painted suntop. The back seat was folded down and made into a carrier, which held scuba diving equipment. A black diving suit, still dripping wet, was hanging from one of the suntop support struts.

I said, "Oh, I hope I'm not taking you away from your fun?"

Jesse flung my suitcase next to his diving tank, saying, "No. I'm done diving for the day."

As he started the motor, I said, "I appreciate your picking me up, Jesse."

"I told you, I'm done and I'm going home," he said impatiently.

As we drove through the unspoiled little town, I didn't detect many changes since my last visit about three years prior. There were still no signs of any chain establishments, just little shops, boutiques and restaurants, most of which had outdoors seating options.

I was musing at Avalon's history for a few moments. William Wrigley Jr., the chewing gum baron, purchased Santa Catalina Island from the Banning brothers in 1919. He set to work to develop Catalina with the same gusto that had prompted his success in business. Mr. Wrigley hoped that the island would become a year-round vacation spot. Seeking employment for the local population, he established a pottery and tile plant, as well as a furniture factory. He also built a reservoir for the island's water supply. The most famous and spectacular sight to Mr. Wrigley's credit on the island was the casino building. The building had become the landmark of Catalina ever since its creation in the year 1929.

Soon we had left the village behind and were heading up a steep, curvy hill. As we gained in altitude, the view to the town below and the ocean beyond was simply breathtaking. I was reminded of old fishing villages in Italy or Spain.

I turned to Jesse and said, "This place is paradise!"

He replied, "I guess so. But except for diving, it's pretty boring here."

"I'll admit, when I was your age, I was not particularly interested in scenery either," I said.

He gave me a look which indicated that he doubted I could ever have been his age.

As the golf cart climbed higher on the steep wavy road, I noticed a few driveways leading to homes, with ample space between each house. Following a few more curves in the road, we turned down a driveway on the south side of the street and stopped in front of a house. The architectural style of the villa was a mixture of Spanish and Mediterranean, judging by the stucco exterior, the tile roof and the entryway arches.

Jesse commented, "We're here."

I said, "Home, sweet home!"

He just rolled his eyes and pushed the remote control button of his garage opener. We drove into the garage where two other identical golf carts were already parked, except their suntops had been painted different colors. One was red, the other yellow. Jesse parked the green one, adding to the collection.

He wanted to help me with the suitcase again, but I pulled it off the carrier and said, "I'll take it. It's not very heavy and it has wheels. You take care of your equipment and wetsuit. Thanks for the ride."

As we approached the front door, a woman in her early thirties opened it to us. She was wearing jeans and a white cotton button-down shirt, which flattered her compact, well-proportioned body. Her wavy brown hair was neatly pulled back and tied at her nape. The woman gave the impression of being self-assured and confident.

She said, "Hi Jesse," and as she turned to me, I was briefly scrutinized by a pair of hazel eyes. Then she smiled and said, "You must be Mrs. Huber. Welcome! I'm Beatrix Primrose, the housekeeper. I'm sure you first want to unpack and change into something more comfortable. Come, I'll show you to your room."

I felt perfectly comfortable in what I had on, a pair of cropped navy slacks and a navy and white sailor top, but I wasn't going to argue with her.

Jesse said, "See you," and vanished down the hall.

Ms Primrose grabbed my bag and I followed her up the stairs. I thought to myself, I must look feeble; nobody lets me carry my own luggage.

She led me to a room on the second story, and opening the door, she said, "Here you are."

Stepping inside, I exclaimed, "Oh, it's beautiful! I hope I'm not inconveniencing anyone?"

Ms Primrose replied, "Not at all. There are five bedrooms on this floor. Gina's is the one next to yours. The one beyond hers is Jesse's. If Tony and his wife come to visit, they can use the guest room across the hall, and my room is at the very end of the corridor. The master bedroom is downstairs, and if Guido happens to come while you're here, he'll also sleep downstairs in the den."

Then she said, "All right. I'll leave you alone now so you can get settled in. If you need anything, just holler."

Left by myself, I surveyed the room. It was all done in pastels. The quilt, spread out over the queen- size bed, was crafted in a geometrical design of baby blues, lilacs and white. The curtains and bed-skirt depicted the various shades of lilac used in the quilt. The dresser, nightstand and desk all looked to be solid oak. I also found a roomy walk-in closet. A connecting door led into a bathroom, also done in blue and lilac. All the walls were painted white.

I opened the sliding-glass door and stepped out onto a balcony. Wow! I had an ocean view! A little white wicker table with two matching chairs was set up on the balcony. I opted not to sit and enjoy the view just then. I did not want to linger in my room for too long. After all, I hadn't even come across Millie at that point.

Unpacking only took me a few minutes. Most of the clothing I had packed was casual. Some shorts, comfortable pants and tops, a few summer frocks, and yes, the essential, prepared-for-anything simple little black dress. Having finished putting away my clothes and shoes in the closet, I could not decide where to store the .25 caliber pistol and ammo. Not knowing how long my visit would take, I figured that the room would probably be cleaned at some point, and I did not want to advertise my gun. Eventually I made up my mind. I took all my toilet articles out of the make-up bag and stored them in the bathroom. Then I placed the pistol in the empty make-up bag, which I tossed into the empty suitcase. I then stored the suitcase at the very back of the walk-in closet. The ammunition I rolled up in a pair of panties, which I tucked in between other underwear.

Thus, "settled in," as the housekeeper put it, I left my room and descended the stairs. Standing in the entry hall once more, I did not see nor hear anyone.

Since I was told to "holler," I obliged and yelled, "Hello! Ms Primrose!"

The housekeeper came out of a room down the hall, saying "Yes?"

"Sorry to disturb you, Ms Primrose. Is my friend at home?"

"Yes, Mrs. Faracelli is here. She's working on a sculpture. I'll show you where her studio is. And please call me Beatrix."

"Oh, I don't want to interrupt her."

Beatrix said, "She doesn't mind. She told me she wanted to see you as soon as you're ready, Mrs. Huber."

I followed the housekeeper through the house and out the back door. About thirty yards away, I noticed a separate structure.

Pointing to it I asked, "Is that it?"

She nodded, and I said, "I'll find her. Thank you, Beatrix."

Chapter 5

◇◇◇◇◇◇◇◇◇◇◇◇◇◇◇◇◇

The door to the studio was ajar, so I pushed it open. I found myself in a large, airy room, with natural lighting coming from all directions. There was a feeling of windows outnumbering walls. To my right, I was looking at canvases of finished and started paintings, as well as easels, palettes, brushes, et cetera. Sculptures were stored on shelves to the left of the door. On a small, round table set apart from the rest stood a bronze of a man's head. The piece of art was about 20 inches tall and made quite an imposing statement. Despite the long hair pulled into a ponytail, the handsome face was decidedly masculine. There was a sink with two enormous tanks at the far end of the room. The most impressive object in the place however, was a huge rectangular workbench in the center of the room, taking up three quarters of the space. Millie sat at the workbench, with tools and materials spread all around her. She was intently concentrated, working on a sculpture, presumably depicting a bird of some kind, and apparently had not heard me come into the room.

I had ample time to study Millie. She had one of those ageless faces. From a distance, she still looked very much like the girl I had known in Fribourg. Blue, wide-set eyes, excellent cheekbones, and straight ash blond hair kept in a blunt cut, ending an inch above her shoulders. Coming closer, I noticed she wore no make-up and that her hair was streaked with gray.

She suddenly rubbed her hands. Then, looking up, she exclaimed, "Reg! How wonderful to see you!" And she added, "I can't touch you, I'm filthy."

I rushed at her anyhow, and embracing her tightly, I said, "Millie, it is great to be here!" Then I said, "Nobody had called me 'Reg' in ages until I ran into Lillie the other day. I am getting used to it again, and I like it!"

She said, "What do people call you nowadays?"

I replied, "Professionally I'm known as R. A. Huber. Peter and my friends call me Regula."

Millie said, "Oh yes, Regula. I've never liked that name. Sounds like a frozen dinner to me."

She got up from behind the workbench, walked over to the sink and washed her hands thoroughly, wiped them dry, and then said, "Now I'm ready for a good chat with you."

I said, "Please don't stop working on the sculpture on my account. We can talk while you work."

She replied, "My hands need a rest. Besides, it's getting close to lunch time."

Then she asked, "Do you and Peter still live in Merida?"

"Yes. We love it there. We are both retired and manage to keep busy. Peter's hobby is writing, and I opened a little business in Pasadena."

"Is Peter any good?"

I stared at her.

She laughed and said, "I mean, is he any good as a writer? Whether or not he's any good at other things is between him and you!"

I burst out laughing and said, "It sure is good to see you, Millie, and you haven't changed a bit!"

Then I said, "I think Peter shows talent in his writing, but I don't want you to take him on as your next protégé. That might prove dangerous!"

She giggled and said, "You might be right! I've heard about your little business. You're a private eye. I can imagine you're excellent at it."

I replied, "I have been lucky so far. I was able to solve some intriguing cases."

"Luck had nothing to do with it. You've always been good at snooping."

I raised my eyebrows, "Somehow that does not sound like a compliment."

She said, "Oh, but it is. I'm thinking of our 'Three Musketeers' days at the boarding school. Remember when several students' little personal items were disappearing? You solved the mystery and figured out who the thief was."

"Well," I said, "That was in self defense; I had been the suspect and of course had to clear my name."

"Of course!"

Then she said, "Lillie mentioned that you've been working too hard and that you needed a break. Catalina is the perfect place for you to relax."

I replied, "Yes. I've been to the island several times before, and I loved each visit. Thanks for inviting me."

Millie rubbed her hands again, walked over to the sink, took a glass and a vial of what looked like prescription medication from the cabinet above, dropped a pill into her mouth, and washed it down with a drink of water.

I said, " Are you ill?"

She replied, "Not really. I suffer from arthritis in my hands. One of these"-- she pointed at the medication - - "usually helps stop the pain."

I said, "OK, Millie, let's talk about you. I hear there is new excitement in your life!"

"What did you hear?"

"Oh, just that you made a new discovery, namely a painter."

Millie said, "Yes. I want to tell you about Michael. You'll like him. I'll tell you over lunch."

I followed her out of the studio.

Back in the house, we found the housekeeper in the laundry room, ironing a pair of slacks.

Millie said, "When you get a chance, Beatrix, can you fix us some lunch?"

"Of course, Mrs. Faracelli. Turkey sandwiches OK, or shall I fix a salad?"

Millie looked at me, "Sandwich OK?"

I said, "Perfectly."

Then she announced, "We'll eat out on the patio," and I followed her down the hallway, through a large living room, and out onto a covered veranda.

Chapter 6

◇◇◇◇◇◇◇◇◇◇◇◇◇◇◇◇◇

On the veranda, I admired the ocean view once more. We had barely settled into the comfortable patio chairs facing each other across the table when Beatrix brought our sandwiches and lemonade.

After she was out of earshot, I commented, "She is very fast! She seems competent as well."

Millie said, "Beatrix is an absolute jewel. I don't know what I'd do without her."

I said, "She does not strike me as your average domestic help."

"No. She is quite unusual. She has a college degree but prefers to be a housekeeper. I pay her a handsome salary, but she's worth every penny. She's an excellent cook, cleans, does laundry and ironing, does the shopping, et cetera. In other words, she runs the household. She is a godsend!"

I said, "A regular *Mary Poppins*!"

"Good comparison!"

"How did you find her?"

"Through an employment agency."

"Has she been with you long?"

Millie replied, "Oh, about two and a half years. My last housekeeper, Angelica, was getting up in age and went back to her native Chile to retire. She saved quite a bit of money, which enables her to live in that country comfortably for the rest of her life, including having her own maid. I was happy for her, of course, but hated to lose her."

I said, "A good housekeeper is not easy to come by."

"Exactly. That's why I feel so fortunate to have Beatrix. The agency had highly recommended her, but she has surpassed all my expectations."

Lunch over with, and the dishes cleared away, I pulled out my cigarettes and lighter.

Millie said, "You still smoke?"

I replied, "You disapprove?"

"Oh, no. We all have our vices. I'm just surprised, your being so athletic and all."

"I'm trying to cut down."

Then I said, "You were going to tell me about Michael."

She complied, "I met him down in the village one day. I was coming off the boat, and there he was, having his paintings spread out on the sidewalk, trying to sell them. I glanced at his work in passing and was very much impressed. I could tell right away that he was extremely talented. I bought one of his paintings, a still-life. He told me that the paintings displayed on the sidewalk were just small samples of his work. He lived on the mainland and could only transport a small portion of his art. I told him I might be interested in seeing more of his work. He gave me his card, and that was that."

I said, "When was this?"

"Oh, I guess in March or April."

She continued, "About two weeks later, I happened to be in his neighborhood, and I stopped by to look at the rest of his paintings. Reg, some of them are absolutely fabulous! Anyhow, that's how I met Michael. At first I was only interested in him as an artist, but then the interest became more personal. By the way, we are putting an exhibit together for him. It will be held this Saturday at the Casino Ballroom."

"That's only three days away!"

"I know. Michael is meeting with the art exhibits coordinator, as we speak. I believe she will come here tomorrow and help make the final decisions about which artworks will be chosen for the exhibit."

I said, "Michael lives here with you. Correct?"

Millie grinned and said, "You bet!"

Then she looked at me pensively, and said, "You've been happily married to the same man for forty years, haven't you?"

"Yes," I replied, "There have been ups and downs as in all marriages, but overall, they've been good years."

She said, "If Anthony hadn't been killed, I'm sure we'd still be married today. After all these years, I find myself still missing him."

I asked, "Do you feel that your last two husbands had taken advantage of you?"

"Not at all," she replied. "I got what I wanted out of the marriages. Besides, I got a kick out of helping them with their careers."

"I see."

Millie said, "Richard, alias Rico Ramono, was a lot of fun to be with. Like most opera singers, he was very temperamental. When happy, the house echoed with his laughter; when upset, it vibrated from the outbursts of his scorn. I knew how to handle him, and we had two good years together."

She laughed and said, "He used to walk around the house and garden practicing his scales between octaves. You can imagine with what force he used his vocal cords!"

I inquired, "Did you know he was gay when you married him?"

"No. He was actually still fighting it himself."

"Oh."

"When I came to realize what his tormenting fight within himself was all about, I suggested he should accept and live what he is, rather than what he would like to be."

I said, "I admire you for your tolerance, Millie."

She replied, "Oh, it was just a fact of life."

"How about your last husband, Jason Limburg?"

A sad expression appeared on Millie's face, and she said, "Looking back, I think I've failed Jason in many ways. I knew he was sensitive and not very strong emotionally. I did not realize it at the time, but I think I pushed him into success he wasn't able to handle. Being excited about his talent -- and believe me, he was enormously talented -- I failed to recognize the signs of stress he showed. When he started to drink heavily, I should have known. One day, he took off without a word to his son or me. That was five years ago. No one seems to have heard from him since. We don't know where he is and if he's alive or dead. I hired people to trace him, but without results."

I said, "Millie, I hope you are not blaming yourself for this?"

"Well, I should have been more sensitive to his needs at the time."

I asked, "Did you get a divorce from him, or are you still legally married?"

"I filed for 'divorce by desertion,' or whatever it is called, this May. I figured, after five years, it was time. Jason is either dead or lives incognito in some remote country. Even Jesse has given up hope of ever hearing from his father. The boy was optimistic in the first couple of years that his dad might be found."

I said, "I met Jesse. He picked me up at the harbor. I got the impression that this young man is harboring a lot of anger and resentment."

Millie said, "Yes. Poor Jesse does not have it easy."

And she proceeded to tell me all about the teenager's past and recent troubles. I did not let on that her twin sister had already informed me about all this.

After her narrative came to an end, I asked, "How is Jesse doing now?"

"He's getting there, I think. There has been no more trouble with drugs. His tutor is positive he can get him caught up with his schoolwork. Jesse has been taking scuba diving lessons the last few weeks, and seems to love it."

Then I inquired, "How are your other children doing? I take it they're all well established in their professions by now?"

She replied, " They should be, but every one of them seems to be in financial difficulty."

"Oh?"

"Tony is a pilot and got laid off. He has not been able to find another job, which is no surprise, considering what the airline industry is like today.

"Gina is a model. At age 34, her modeling career is virtually over. She still looks great, but in her business, youth is all that counts. She is engaged to a local doctor here on the island.

"Guido is a born entrepreneur. Unfortunately, he is also a gambler. He gambled his first business away and is now on the verge of losing his second."

I said, "Sorry to hear all that."

Millie sighed, "I think I've made the mistake of always helping them out. They could always come to Mother as their financial resource. Consequently, they've never learned to rely on themselves. I won't live forever, and the children will have to learn to stand on their own two feet."

I said, "Do the children like Michael?"

She answered, "They like him well enough, but they're worried that I might marry him."

"They wouldn't like that?"

She shook her head. "I think they're afraid I might cut them out of the will. A thing I'd never do, of course."

I said, "Will you?"

"Will I what?"

"Marry him?"

"I don't know yet. In the meantime, I'll just live in sin!"

Then she said, "Now Reg, tell me, are you comfortable here?"

I said, "Absolutely. My room is wonderful, and the view from the balcony is breathtaking!"

"Anytime you want to go someplace, take the red golf cart. It's mine, and since I'm the one that goes down to the village least often, we'll share it."

"I noticed three different-colored golf carts parked in the garage," I said.

Millie replied, "We actually have five. Michael's is blue, Gina uses the pink one, and Jesse drives the green one, as you know. The yellow is for Beatrix, and as I said, the red is mine and now yours."

"Millie, how organized you are!"

"You know darned well, I've never been organized, and never will be, for that matter! The only organized person in this house is Beatrix."

"So it was Beatrix's idea to paint the carts different colors?"

Millie said, "No. Actually it was Michael's idea. Pretty clever, huh? Let me explain. I used to confuse the golf carts. After all, they all looked the same. I would try to start the carts with the wrong keys all the time, which was frustrating."

I interrupted, "The keys could have all been left in the ignitions, while the carts were parked in the garage."

She said, "Yes. We used to do it that way. With all the people coming and going all summer, we are pretty negligent. Sometimes carts are left in the driveway, or the garage door stays open. Anyhow, last summer, a couple of 12-year-old boys living in the neighborhood at the time took one of our golf carts for a joyride down the hill. Luckily they did not get hurt, but I would probably have been liable had anything happened to them. Since that time, we always make sure the keys are not left in the ignitions."

She continued, "As I said, I always managed to get hold of the wrong cart. Once, I even tried to start some stranger's vehicle, parked next to mine, in the village. The man came out of a store, saying, 'Lady, are you trying to steal my cart?' It was embarrassing.

"So, shortly after Michael moved in, he painted the golf carts different colors, and he also color-coordinated the keys. Wasn't that clever of him?"

I said, "I'm impressed!" And I added, "I can't wait to meet Michael!"

Millie said, "He should get home in the late afternoon or early evening."

Then she said, "You'll have to excuse me for a while. I try to take a little nap every day. Feel free to explore the house and grounds. In other words, make yourself at home, Reg."

Chapter 7

◇◇◇◇◇◇◇◇◇◇◇◇◇◇◇◇◇◇

I took Millie up on her suggestion and started by exploring the outdoor property. From the veranda a path led around each side of the house. I took the walkway heading east, in the direction of the studio. A border of purple and yellow pansies was planted along each side of the path. To my right, stepping stones led towards a rose garden. As I left the studio structure behind, the hillside ahead looked wild and rugged. There was no more evidence of careful landscaping. The area seemed left to its natural vegetation of trees and shrubs. I noticed an Ironwood tree, which I am positive is extinct in most other places. I spotted some California Holly and patches of St. Catherine's Lace, already turning a light brown color.

I came to a junction where the path branched out. I could either go straight or turn left where stepping stones led up a steep mound. I chose the trail straight forward. A few yards ahead, I noticed a sort of balcony overhead, formed by a natural ledge in the massive rock formation. As I walked along the undercut of this formation, I could hear the echo of my footsteps. I guessed that, had I taken the path to the left earlier, it would have guided me to that ledge above.

I walked on, enjoying the tranquility and peace of nature around me, until I came to the end of the trail. I found myself by a tall hedge, evenly shaped, apparently separating Millie's property from the next estate. On the other side of the hedge, I spotted a treehouse sticking up above the ground, and beyond that a large home. I turned and headed back.

The path forked and separated from that direction as well. This time I chose the "high road." As the trail led up a steep little hill, I realized I was climbing up to the ledge. Arriving at the top, I was enchanted. A wooden bench had been placed to one side of the platform. At the very edge of the overhang, an iron balustrade had been erected for safety. I leaned on the railing and drank in the view. I was surrounded by hillsides, and far below, I beheld Avalon and the blue waters beyond.

I stood for a while, watching a ship sailing on the horizon. Then I slowly turned and made my way back to civilization.

Chapter 8

◇◇◇◇◇◇◇◇◇◇◇◇◇◇◇◇◇

I met Michael at dinner on my first evening on the island. There were five of us seated at the large table in the dining room: Millie, Michael, Gina, Jesse and me. At first, the conversation focused on the upcoming art exhibit. Michael explained all the arrangements the coordinator, Pamela Norris, and he had made that day. They had selected numerous works among his paintings left in storage on the mainland. Pamela would arrange for them to be professionally transported to Avalon on Friday morning.

Millie turned to Michael and said, "I hope you stood your ground and did not let her make all the choices?"

He replied, "I put my foot down once or twice, but basically Pamela made most of the decisions about what works are being exhibited. After all, she's the expert of what draws the public's interest."

Michael then elaborated on additional arrangements done that day. Back on the island, they had talked to the person in charge of the Casino Ballroom. It was decided that all the art works would be transported and set up at the ballroom on Friday. Pamela and her professional team would take care of this. The next day, Thursday, the coordinator would come to the property and choose the paintings kept in the house and studio. She would also choose a few of Millie's sculptures.

At the mention of her sculptures, Millie cringed and said, "I've told Pamela before, I don't want any of my sculptures shown. This is your exhibit, Michael!"

He replied, "You'll have to take that up with her yourself, tomorrow."

During Michael's narrative, I looked at the faces around me. Michael himself seemed modestly concentrated on his subject. He addressed us all, but he kept his dark brown eyes mainly fixed on Millie. I would have recognized his face as that of the bronze in Millie's studio even if his long hair hadn't been tied into a ponytail. There was a sense of charm about him; nevertheless, I felt he was basically a shy man. Millie seemed completely absorbed in his words. Jesse looked totally bored. Gina focused on her plate, busily shoving aside all foods high in calories.

Then Millie addressed Jesse, saying, "How did your diving lesson go today?"

Jesse perked up and replied, "Great! The instructor said that I'd be ready to get my certification soon."

Millie said, "Good for you, Jesse!"

Gina eyed me across the table, saying, "I remember you from when I was a kid. You gave me a Barbie outfit you had sewn yourself, as a birthday present."

I said, "Imagine, you still remember that!"

"Oh, they were the most fabulously chic clothes my Barbie ever wore! A cream silk blouse, a fawn wool skirt, a black leather jacket with matching boots, and to top the ensemble off, an enormous fawn hat!"

Chuckling, I said, "I can see the outfit made a big hit, for you to remember every detail after all these years!"

Beatrix came to clear the dishes away.

I said, "That was an excellent dinner, Beatrix, thank you very much."

She said, "Glad you enjoyed it." And looking at Michael, she added, "If the soufflé was overdone, it's because dinner was delayed."

That said, she gathered her tray and left the room.

Michael grimaced and said to the closing door, "Well, sorry for upsetting your schedule. Next time I make the crossing, I'll tell the captain to put the boat in full throttle!"

Gina got up and said, "Excuse me, everyone. I'm going down to see Charles for a while."

Turning to me, she said, "Hope you'll enjoy your vacation on the island, Mrs. Huber."

Michael excused himself as well, saying, "I feel restless. I'm going for a walk." And bending over Millie, kissing her, he added, "I'll be back soon."

Jesse just said, "See you," and was gone.

Left by ourselves, Millie said, "So what do you think of Michael?"

I replied, "I like him."

"Just wait until you see his art, Reg. You're in for a treat!"

I asked, "Who is Charles?"

Millie answered, "He is Gina's fiancé. I'm sure you'll meet him while you're here."

"Have they set a date for their wedding yet?"

"Not yet, but I think they are working on it. Charles is very good for Gina. He calms her down. He is the extremely intelligent, logical, even-tempered type. He doesn't take any nonsense from her either."

"What do you mean?" I asked.

Millie smiled and said, "Oh, nothing drastic. Having made a name for herself in the modeling world, Gina is a little spoiled. She is used to having things her way. When faced with opposition, she tends to show her temper. Dr. Charles Timble does not let her 'run' him."

We sat in silence for a while, and then I commented, "I've had a wonderful day here, so far. While you were napping, I took a walk on your grounds. The view from the top of the hill, where you've made a little terrace out of the natural ledge, is magnificent!"

Millie said, "Yes. Up there is my favorite place to relax. We call it the 'lookout.'"

Then I said, "Dinner was great. Beatrix is an excellent cook."

"Yes, she is."

"Does she eat all by herself in the kitchen?"

"Yes. By her own choice. On the mainland, when there was only Jesse and myself, she would join us for meals. Here, especially when there are many people to cook for, she prefers to eat by herself, after everyone else is served. Besides, I don't think she'd be comfortable seated at dinner with Michael."

I said, "Judging from that little episode after dinner, I take it that Beatrix is not a fan of Michael?"

She said, "You are right. They don't like each other."

"Why?"

"I don't really know. They had a strong aversion to one another from the very beginning. Beatrix seems to resent Michael's presence in the house. Michael, for his part, seems to think Beatrix is bossy. I guess they are both protective of me and, consequently, hate each other."

I said, "I see."

Millie continued, "Most of the time, they try to be civil with each other, but every so often, like tonight, their feelings get the better of them."

I had to suppress a yawn and said, "Millie, you'll have to excuse me. I got up at the crack of dawn this morning, and I am suddenly feeling tired. If you don't mind, I'll head up to my room, read for a while, and go to bed."

She replied, "Of course not. Have a good night."

Up in my room, I stepped out on the balcony. The stars above shone brightly, and the lights of Avalon below reflected on the ocean. I sat down in one of the wicker chairs, summing up what I had learned so far on my first day on the island.

Chapter 9

◇◇◇◇◇◇◇◇◇◇◇◇◇◇◇◇◇◇

Thursday morning, I woke up to another day of blue skies and a pleasantly warm temperature.

Coming down the stairs, I headed out to the patio where I found Gina, having breakfast.

Looking around, I said, "Good morning! Where is everyone?"

Gina said, "A good morning to you too, Mrs. Huber!" And she added, "Everyone except us seems to be busy. The art coordinator is already here, putting Mom and Michael hard to work in the office. Bruce Dillon, the tutor, just showed up and is keeping Jesse under control. I'm sure Beatrix is making herself useful someplace in the house."

Looking at my watch, I said, "Oh, it is past nine already. How embarrassing to be the last one to get up!"

Gina replied, "Not at all. You're on vacation." She grinned and added, "I just came down myself. I don't have a job right now, so there's no hurry to get up."

Then she said, "Have some breakfast."

I replied, "Thanks, I don't mind if I do."

A place setting was already laid for me. In the center of the table stood a coffee pot, a pitcher with orange juice, a basket containing toast and rolls, butter, jelly and fruit. I helped myself to all of the above.

Then I said, "I know you are a successful model. Are you in between jobs, or are you permanently giving up modeling?"

She answered, "I'm getting too old for the profession. I've been offered little jobs here and there lately, but basically my career is over."

"Are you planning to look into another line of work?"

"Eventually, I guess I'll have to, but I'm not trained or schooled for anything else."

I studied her carefully. She had a lovely face with high cheekbones, brown eyes, a straight chiseled nose, full lips and a dark shade of auburn hair. When she had walked out of the dining room the night before, I had noticed her typical model body: tall, thin and lanky, a long neck, and legs that seemed to go on forever.

Then I said, "With your looks, you might try your luck in the entertainment business. Some former models have succeeded in that field."

She laughed and said, "The only problem with that is, I can't act, sing, nor dance!"

Finishing my breakfast, I commented, "I heard you are engaged to an MD."

"Yes, I am."

"What kind of doctor is he?"

"He is a G.P. and shares a practice with another doctor in Avalon. He is very interested in doing research, though, and aims at opening his own lab at some point in the future."

"Interesting."

"Unfortunately, that'll take a great deal of funds, which he has no idea how to raise."

I asked, "How did you meet?"

Gina replied, "We met at the New Year's Eve dance held annually at the Catalina Casino Ballroom. We got engaged in April."

"Are you making any wedding plans yet?"

"Well, we haven't set a date yet. It will be sometime in the spring of next year. As far as the planning goes, we kind of have different ideas. Charles would prefer a small, simple wedding, shared with just a few friends and family. I have something more elaborate in mind."

She grinned and stated, "Time will tell who wins our first battle!"

"Well," I said, "I sure enjoyed my breakfast and chatting with you, Gina."

I got up from the table, gathered the empty dishes, and returned them to the kitchen.

Chapter 10

◇◇◇◇◇◇◇◇◇◇◇◇◇◇◇◇◇◇◇

Walking down the hall, I heard voices coming from one of the rooms. The door stood open, so I looked in. The room was large and seemed to be generally used as an office, but on this occasion it looked more like an art showroom. Paintings of a variety of type and size were arranged in every available space. Signs depicting the title were placed underneath each work of art. A woman whom I presumed was the coordinator stood in the center of the room, clipboard and pen in hand. She looked to be in her twenties. She was dressed in a chic beige tailored suit. Her make-up was expertly applied and she kept her light brown hair in a neat short style. The young woman gave the impression of being very much in charge. She was reading off titles and numbers from her list while Michael identified each painting and Millie attached the corresponding numbers to each work. I stood in the doorway and surveyed the scene.

Millie spotted me and said, "Come in, Reg. We are just about done here."

She made the introductions. "This is Pamela Norris, our art exhibits coordinator." And with a gesture in my direction, she said, "Meet my friend, Regula Huber."

Ms Norris briefly looked up from her notes, saying "Hi," then turned back to her task.

While the three of them finished numbering and tagging their objects, I tried not to get in the way, studying some of the paintings closely. Every category of oil painting was represented: landscapes, portraits, still-lifes, nudes, and abstracts. I noticed a few watercolors as well. I am by no means an art expert, but some of Michael's works were decidedly masterpieces.

I addressed Ms Norris, "This might be a dumb question, but what is your reason for numbering them?"

She replied, "This will make it easier to set up at the ballroom. My team of 'muscle men' will professionally pack the paintings, transport them down to Avalon, and place them in the Casino Ballroom for the exhibit. Once there, they'll arrange them in the numbered order, so I don't have to supervise every step they take. Michael and I have already previously made the decisions in which order we'll display his works. I might do some re-arranging on the spot, at my discretion."

Then she said, "We are done in here. Let's go to the studio and choose a few additional paintings stored there, as well as some of your sculptures, Mrs. Faracelli."

Millie said, "I've told you before how I feel about displaying my sculptures at Michael's exhibit! My work has been introduced to the public often enough. This is Michael's show, and I don't want to take away from his credit."

The coordinator said, "Believe me, it will be beneficial to Michael, showing a few of your pieces as well."

Turning to Michael, Millie said, "Say something, Sweetheart. How do you feel about it?"

He answered, "Pamela probably knows best, but it's up to you, my pet, whether or not you'll allow her to show your work."

Pamela Norris ushered us all out of the office, and on the way to the studio said, "Please, let's not waste time. I've done this many times before, and I know what I'm doing. Besides, the write-up has already been released to the press with the statement, 'Some of Mildred Faracelli's sculptures will be displayed.' "

At the studio entrance, I made an attempt at excusing myself, but Millie said, "Oh please, Reg, stay with us."

I said, "Are you sure I won't be in the way?"

"Of course not," she replied.

Ms Norris said, "OK. Here we are. We'll select the additional pieces now and then have them transferred to the office." She first surveyed the paintings stored to the right of the door, one by one, and made her choices. She then walked over to the shelf garnished with sculptures and made her selections there as well.

She looked first at Millie, then Michael, saying, "If these pieces meet with your approval, we'll title and number them right now." She rummaged in her big bag, and out came the clipboard and pen.

I thought to myself, any moment now she'll clap her hands and say, "Come on, children, don't dawdle and get to work!"

Millie must have been thinking along the same lines.

She grimaced and then winked at me, saying, *"Tournons le farceur!"*

Pamela Norris stared and said, "Excuse me?"

Millie said, "Just a joke. Don't mind me."

The coordinator shrugged. Then she pointed at the bronze on the little table, saying, "This is spectacular! You must have done it quite recently."

Millie replied, "Yes, it turned out good. I just got it back from the casters last week."

Ms Norris announced, "We'll place it right at the entrance!"

Millie protested, "You want a head of Michael at his exhibit?"

"Of course, it's perfect!"

Millie exclaimed, "That's absurd!"

Then she turned to Michael and asked, "Do you really want this at your show?"

Michael took some time before he answered, "It is a great piece of art, but I don't know if I like the idea of having it set up right at the entrance. I mean, people might find it arrogant of the painter if the first thing they see at his exhibit is a sculpture of himself."

Pamela Norris exclaimed, "Not at all. Everyone will be delighted!"

Millie looked at me and inquired, "Reg, what do you think?"

I was taken by surprise, thought about it for a minute, then said, "It might be a nice touch. The public can get familiar with the painter's face, as well as appreciate the fine art of the sculpture."

The coordinator exclaimed, "Bravo!"

Millie sighed and turned to Ms Norris, "OK. Have it your way. Personally, I think it shows poor taste, but go ahead and show it in the exhibit."

A triumphant smile on her face, the coordinator said, "Thank you, Mrs. Faracelli, for being so generous."

It took them a few minutes to title, number and tag the art objects.

Then Ms Norris said, "OK, I'll call my team now to transfer everything to the office. They might as well start packing some of the paintings today, and get a head start."

Turning to Michael, she said, "I need to go over a couple more things with you concerning the paintings in storage on the mainland. Can we go sit someplace?"

Michael said, "Sure."

Millie asked, "I hope you don't need me anymore?"

Ms Norris replied, "No, thank you, Mrs. Faracelli. Everything is pretty much under control."

Chapter 11

◇◇◇◇◇◇◇◇◇◇◇◇◇◇◇◇◇◇◇

The door shutting behind the two, Millie sighed with relief and said, "That woman is so organized, she gives me a headache!"

She went to the cabinet above the sink and reached for her medication.

I said, "You pop a pill every time I see you, Millie."

I joined her by the sink and glanced at the vial. The label read, *Sehydrin. Take 3 times a day.* There was no doctor's name listed, which I thought strange.

I then went over to the little table and studied the impressive sculpture once more.

I commented, "You captured Michael's expression well." And I added, "What is this expression, exactly? Love, satisfaction, concentration, regret, or all of the above?"

A mysterious smile brushed her face, and she said, "You are very perceptive, Reg! Not even Michael, himself, is aware of what I've captured."

I looked at her questioningly, but she said no more.

I asked, "Are you going to be busy all day with the preparations for the exhibit?"

She replied, "I think they can do without me from here on."

Then she pointed at her started work of the bird, left on the workbench, saying, "I had planned to work on that today, but now, with the coordinator's men trampling through here at any moment, I think I'll forget about it."

I said, "Explain the mechanics of sculpture to me, Millie. I take it this bird will become a bronze?"

"Eventually, yes," she replied.

I asked, "What's that wooden thing called that your bird seems to be attached to?"

" An armature."

"You're making the sculpture out of clay. Correct?"

"Yes."

"Could you use other materials, besides clay?"

"Yes."

I exclaimed, "Millie, please! Don't give me one-word answers. I really am interested in the process involved in creating a sculpture from start to finish."

She looked at me amused, and said, "So you want to know about the lost wax process; the traditional method of bronze casting? It has been around for over 5000 years, you know!"

"Yes, tell me about it," I begged.

"I warn you, it's complicated!"

"I'll try my best to comprehend it," I said, mockingly.

Millie stated, "OK. You create your sculpture out of clay or plaster over an armature. I personally prefer to work with clay. I like the feel of it" - -

I interrupted, "Is the armature always made from wood?"

She said, "You can use wadded up wire, or wooden dowels like I'm using with this bird, metal or plastic, anything you wish, depending on the shape and size of the piece." And she continued, "I form the basic shape of the sculpture with my hands, adding more clay as needed. For the finer details I use sculpting tools."

Surveying the array of tools scattered on the workbench, I pointed to one with a sharp point and asked, "Is this a stylus?"

"No," she replied, "That's a sgraffito tool."

Millie kept going, "After I'm satisfied with my work, I send it to the foundry for the casting process. I've used the same foundry for years. They're located near San Diego."

I said, "When you talked to Pamela Norris earlier, I heard you mention that you recently got the bronze of Michael back from the casters. Who are the casters?"

She smiled, and said, "Reg, nothing escapes you! Actually the correct term for these businesses is 'foundry.' I call them the casters, because what they do is casting my sculptures for me."

"Could you do the casting yourself?"

"I could," she said, "Actually years ago, I used to do the whole process myself. Now I send it out to be done. It's a very involved process and requires equipment I don't have here on the island. Besides, it's physically strenuous and very messy."

I asked, "So, tell me what they do to your creations at the foundry."

Millie said, "You obviously want to hear the entire procedure. I hope I remember it correctly, step by step.

"Here goes: They first make a flexible rubber mold of the sculpture. Then they remove the clay from the mold and clean it out. Next they tie the mold together and pour wax into it. Then they remove the mold and clean up the seams. After that, they attach vents to the sculpture so that gases can escape when the bronze is poured into the piece.

"Then they invest the piece by making another mold, this time of plaster mixed with grog, around the wax. They then place the investment mold in a burn-out oven to melt the wax out and dry the mold. Next they melt bronze, which is a mixture of copper and small amounts of zinc, tin and lead, in a crucible to a temperature of about 2000 degrees and pour it into the investment mold. After cooling, they tap off the investment mold and remove the vents. Then they sandblast the piece of art to clean the surface from scaling and acids, as well as oils."

Millie continued, "At this stage the casters ship the piece back to me. I then apply a patina to the surface. The last thing I do is polish the bronze to preserve its patina."

She looked at me with a grin on her face, saying, "Voila, now you know it all!"

I said, "Thanks for the lesson, Millie!" And I added, "You were right. Although fascinating, the process of bronze casting sounds very complicated. I don't blame you for shipping that part of the work out. After all, you must get your main satisfaction from creating the piece of art with your hands."

"Exactly," Millie agreed.

After a pause, she said, "Tomorrow Tony and Lisa will come for a few days' visit."

I commented, "I'm looking forward to seeing Tony again and meeting his wife." And I inquired, "How long have they been married?"

"Three years. Lisa is seven months' pregnant."

"You are going to be a grandma, Millie. Congratulations!"

At that moment, the "team" burst in on us, and we left the studio.

Chapter 12

◇◇◇◇◇◇◇◇◇◇◇◇◇◇◇◇◇◇◇

After lunch, Millie excused herself and went to the master bedroom for a nap. Michael and the coordinator were taking off with the "team" to go back down to Avalon, where more arrangements had to be made for the big event on Saturday.

Since I was here to snoop, I decided to check the garage and see who was on the premises. I found only two golf carts parked, the red and the green. Michael, of course, had just left with his blue one. The pink and the yellow carts were also missing. Gina, as well as the housekeeper, was not at home. Walking out of the garage, I noticed a golf cart parked in the driveway. This cart looked to be of a different model and the suntop on it was not painted. I wondered who the visitor could be.

Back in the house, walking down the hall to explore some of the downstairs rooms I had not previously been in, I heard shouting coming from one of them. When I was level with it, I realized the door stood open and I witnessed a little scene.

Jesse was stamping his foot, shaking a folder in his hand, yelling, "Who cares about algebra and geometry anyhow! I'll never need to know about this stuff in real life!"

The man on the other side of the desk patiently replied, "You will need it to get into a good college."

Jesse shouted, "I don't want to go to college! Leave me alone!"

And he jumped out of his chair, flung the folder at the man, and rushed out of the room, almost knocking me over in the hallway. The sheets of papers had fallen out of the folder and were scattered all over the desk and floor.

The man bent down and, with the patience of a saint, picked up the worksheets one by one, carefully ordering them back into the folder. I judged him to be in his late twenties. He was tall and lanky, had a narrow face, wore gold-rimmed glasses, and sported a prominent Adam's apple. He looked up and noticed me standing in the hall.

I introduced myself, "Hello. I am Regula Huber, Mildred Faracelli's friend."

He said, "Hi, Mrs. Huber. Come on in. I am Jesse's tutor, Bruce Dillon."

I sat down on the chair just vacated by Jesse and said, "I'm sorry I witnessed Jesse's outburst. Does he often have temper tantrums?"

Mr. Dillon replied, "When I first started tutoring him, Jesse had frequent temper outbursts, but it happens very seldom now."

I said, "It does not seem to faze you."

He smiled and said, "If it would, I'd have picked the wrong profession."

"Is tutoring your full-time job?"

"No. I'm a high school teacher. During the school year I sometimes take tutoring jobs evenings, and in the summer I can be flexible, of course."

"How big is the high school here on the island? I would assume there are not a great number of students?"

He replied, "I don't know. I think you misunderstood. I don't teach at the school on Catalina. My high school is on the mainland."

I said, "I see."

Then I asked, "How often do you tutor Jesse?"

"Three days a week."

"I hope you've been offered a special rate, having to travel to and from the island three times a week!"

The young man laughed and said, "Even with a special price, that would cost a bundle. Actually, I live on the island for the summer. When I was offered this tutoring job, I jumped at the chance to have a vacation on Catalina on the side. My wife and I rented a room with a kitchenette in town."

I said, "What a great idea, to combine work and pleasure. How long have you been married?"

"Since the beginning of June."

I exclaimed, "So you are actually on an extended honeymoon here. Congratulations!"

My last remark seemed to embarrass him, so I changed the subject and asked, "An occasional temper tantrum aside, how is Jesse doing scholastically?"

"He is coming along pretty good. He was lagging behind practically a whole school year when we started five weeks ago. He is an intelligent young man and I can help him catch up in time for his senior year of high school. I have him just about ready to take his S.A.T. test. When I first met Jesse, he seemed to have a total lack of motivation. I've tried to inspire him, making the learning process interesting and worthwhile. He has come a long way and still has a long way to go, but I am positive he'll be up to date by September. Having a little relapse now and then, like you witnessed today, has to be expected."

I said, "Well, Mr. Dillon, judging from what I've observed and learned in this room, Jesse is in good hands, having an understanding and caring tutor like you."

Realizing I had gotten the man embarrassed again, I quickly added, "I've enjoyed chatting with you, Mr. Dillon. Take care." And I left him.

Chapter 13

◇◇◇◇◇◇◇◇◇◇◇◇◇◇◇◇◇◇◇

I woke up early Friday morning and felt an urge to be physically active. At home, I worked out at the gym regularly, so I needed to find an activity on the island to keep my body and mind agile.

I threw on a pair of shorts, a tee shirt and sneakers, placed wallet, cigarettes and lighter in my fanny pack, and was out my door.

Coming down the stairs, I realized the rest of the household was not up yet. I tiptoed into the kitchen and poured myself a glass of orange juice. There was notepaper and a pen on the counter, and I quickly wrote: "Good morning, Millie. Am taking advantage of your offer and borrowing your golf cart. Going for a jog. Will have breakfast in town. So long, Reg."

I left the note on the dining room table. The keys were hanging on hooks next to the door leading into the garage. I grabbed the red key and was on my way.

When playing golf, I prefer to walk the course, but on a few occasions, I have driven a golf cart. They are very simple to handle. A golf cart does not "idle." Every time you come to a complete stop, the engine also stops. It will start again by stepping on the gas pedal. There are no gears, only one forward and one backward position. The brake pedal consists of two parts: one to stop and one to lock the cart for parking.

Driving the cart down the steep and curvy road gave me a little bit of a rush. Not nearly as much as a downhill ski rush, but good enough! There was no one else on the road so early in the morning; I had the "run" all to myself.

I parked in the center of Avalon on the main drag. The little town looked deserted. I had not bothered to put on my wristwatch, but I judged it to be way before 8 o'clock.

I did a few warm-up exercises by the beach and then started my jog on the walkway towards the Casino.

While jogging, I tried to empty my mind, concentrating solely on my breathing. Arriving at the Casino, I jogged around it in a full circle, and then headed back. At the beach, I turned onto the Green Pleasure Pier and decreased my jog to a fast walk. I rested on a bench for a while before continuing my run toward the docks and back.

When I had reached the village once more, I noticed a restaurant just opened to the public. I waited until my breathing slowed down to normal and then entered to have breakfast. I was the first patron to be seated that morning. Being famished, I ordered coffee, orange juice, ham omelet and hash brown potatoes. As I enjoyed my excellent omelet, I realized a large throng of hungry folks had suddenly gathered around me.

Thus satisfied, I hiked up a hill to explore some of the neat and trim houses further up the slope. On my return, the sleepy little town was coming to life. I browsed through the small stores and boutiques. I was just checking things out. I imagined that I might do some serious shopping in the future. Coming upon a florist, I purchased a bouquet of yellow and white carnations for Millie. Then I decided it was time to head "home."

Driving back up the mountain, I felt proud of myself. I had packed the cigarettes, just in case, but had been able to resist the temptation while down in Avalon.

Rounding the last bend in the road, Millie's house coming into view, I was aware that preparations for the art exhibit the following day were in full swing. There was a big van parked in the driveway, and coming closer, I noticed that Pamela Norris's team was busy carrying artworks out of the house and stowing them in the vehicle.

I parked the golf cart in the garage and returned the key on its hook. I could not find a vase in the kitchen, so I left the flowers in the sink. Then I headed for my room and the shower.

Chapter 14

◇◇◇◇◇◇◇◇◇◇◇◇◇◇◇◇◇◇◇

In mid-afternoon, Tony and his wife arrived. I was seated out on the patio, reading the paper, when they came and joined me.

I looked up at the young man and exclaimed, "Tony, how nice to see you!" And I added, "You startled me. For a brief second I thought I was looking at your father! You are the spitting image of him!"

He replied, "That's what everyone tells me." Then he said, "Meet my wife, Lisa."

And turning to her, he said, "This is Mrs. Huber, Mom's friend."

We all shook hands. I was studying them both. They made a handsome couple. Tony, with his Italian good looks, wavy black hair and dark brown eyes, made a complementary contrast to his fair, blue-eyed spouse. She had Nordic features typically found in persons of Scandinavian decent; light blue eyes, a well shaped nose, and straight, long, naturally blond hair framed her face.

Lisa, clearly pregnant, looked tired, and I asked her, "Can I get you something to drink?"

She replied, "Oh no. Thanks. We just had lunch in town." And she added, "If you don't mind, I'll go upstairs, unpack, and take a short nap."

Tony said, "Good idea. Lisa. See you later."

Left alone with Tony, I said, "Did you actually remember me, or did your mother tell you I was here?"

He answered, "I haven't even seen Mom yet, since we got here. She's probably hiding from the art coordinator woman and all the professional packers running around in the house."

He grinned, adding, "Of course I remember you, Mrs. Huber!"

I replied, "I'm flattered that you still remember me from your childhood."

"I wasn't a child last time I saw you. It was only ten years ago, and I was 26 at the time."

Surprised, I said, "That must have been at your mom's and aunt's 50th birthday party. But Tony, there were about 200 people attending that event! How could you possibly remember me amongst all the crowd?"

He laughed and said, "You made a big impression on me on the dance floor. I had asked Mom at the time, 'Who is that lady with the great rhythm?'"

Chuckling, I said, "My family calls me the dancing queen!"

At that moment Beatrix showed up and offered us refreshments.

Then she said, "Thank God Ms Norris and her minions are just about done here and will leave us in peace."

Tony asked her, "Where is Mom?"

She replied, "She is in her room. The coordinator kept her busy all morning, so she was ready for a nap right after lunch."

Tony got up, saying, "I'll go up and check on Lisa. See you later."

Beatrix asked me, "I take it you're not the napping kind, Mrs. Huber?"

"No. I can't sleep during the day. I sleep deep, like a baby, all night long, though."

She looked at her watch and said, "Already time to start getting dinner organized."

I followed her into the kitchen, saying, "You have another two extra people on your hands. Please let me help with preparing dinner."

Beatrix replied, "Thanks for offering, but that's really not necessary."

I insisted, "Please let me give you a hand. I don't know what to do with myself for the rest of the afternoon anyhow."

The housekeeper eyed me searchingly, and then said, "Oh, all right. If you're really all that bored, go ahead." Then she smiled. "I'm just throwing lasagna together and will stick it in the oven later. You can boil the water for the noodles while I get some of the other ingredients ready."

The kitchen was big and very well organized, so we were not in each other's way. After setting the big pot of water on the stove, I started washing lettuce and vegetables, chopping garlic and parsley while Beatrix was sautéing the meat and preparing the sauce.

We worked in silence for a while, and then I said, "I understand you have a college degree?"

She replied, "Yes. Originally I aimed at a nursing career and took a lot of medical classes. Then I changed course and ended up with a degree in home economics. I earn more money as a housekeeper here than if I would have pursued a career as teacher."

"Did you ever teach?"

"Oh yes. I taught cooking, sewing, embroidery and knitting at a junior college."

Then I asked, "Do you have a boyfriend?"

She glanced at me sideways, and I could tell she was thinking that I was a nosy old woman. I was prepared for an answer of "none of your business."

She must have changed her mind, because she said, "Yes. He's on an African Safari, as we speak."

I inquired, "You could not take time off from your busy job to join him?"

She gave me an impatient look and said, "I'm not particularly interested in the wilds."

At that moment I was sure she regretted having told me about a boyfriend in the first place.

I said, "With all your assets, you might make someone an excellent wife."

"What assets?"

"Cooking, sewing, knitting, et cetera, not to mention above average good looks!"

"Oh, thank you!" And she almost blushed.

I changed the subject, saying, "I could not help but noticing the other night that you and Michael Albertis dislike each other. Why is that?"

She said, " He is taking advantage of Mrs. Faracelli, who is crazy about him."

"He seems to be quite a talented artist, though," I commented.

Beatrix admitted, "I grant you that. If Mrs. Faracelli kept her interest in him strictly as an artist, I could understand, but she did not have to invite him to live with her."

"From what I have observed, he seems to treat Millie well."

She shrugged her shoulder, and said, "He knows on which side his bread is buttered."

By that time all the ingredients were combined and ready for arranging the lasagna in the baking dish. Beatrix alternately layered the noodles, ricotta cheese filling, mozzarella cheese and the meat sauce, finishing with some extra mozzarella. I had made the salad ready, except for the dressing.

The housekeeper looked at her watch and said, "Not quite time yet to bake it in the oven." And she added, "Thank you, Mrs. Huber, for all your help."

I felt myself dismissed.

Chapter 15

◇◇◇◇◇◇◇◇◇◇◇◇◇◇◇◇◇◇◇

At dinner that evening, Millie pointed at the carnations arranged in a vase as the table centerpiece and exclaimed, "Where did these come from?"

I said, "That's the least I can do to show my appreciation for your kind hospitality, Millie."

She replied, "Oh, Reg, they are lovely! You remembered that carnations are my favorite flowers! Thank you very much."

We had barely started to eat the delicious lasagna when Michael's cell phone rang.

After finishing his conversation, he told us, "I need to go down to the ballroom. Apparently some of the paintings taken out of storage have no titles. Pamela does not want to title them without my approval. I'd better hurry. They want to lock up the ballroom soon."

He gulped his dinner down and then excused himself.

The door closing behind him, Lisa said, "This coordinator seems to take herself very seriously."

Millie commented, "Yes. But we have to give her credit; she is good at her job. Nothing gets by her."

Tony turned to his stepmother and said enthusiastically, "Mom, as I told you on the phone, we have to discuss the plan about starting my own flight company. I have it all figured out. I'm sure it will be successful. All I need, of course, is a little capital to start with. And - -"

Millie interrupted his flow, "Tony, not now. We'll discuss it after the exhibit is over. I can't concentrate on anything else at the moment."

Tony, clearly frustrated, said, "I guess you have your priorities. Maybe we shouldn't have come until after this damn exhibit is over and done with."

Lisa gently touched her husband's hand, saying, "Now, Tony. We'll all enjoy the art show tomorrow. Your proposition can wait."

Millie sent a thankful glance in her direction.

Gina commented, "Charles and I are certainly looking forward to it." And turning to me, she inquired, "How about you, Mrs. Huber?"

I said, "I'm sure it will be a treat." Smiling, I added, "Looks like I'm getting to meet your doctor tomorrow as well."

I looked over at Jesse. The boy seemed totally bored with the conversation, and he helped himself to more lasagna.

I asked him, "When is your next diving lesson?"

His face lit up, and he replied, "On Monday. I can't wait!"

"Jesse, you'll have to tell me about your diving experiences one day. I know nothing about the sport and would love to get informed."

"Sure," he said, "if you're really interested, I'll tell you."

"It's a deal," I said enthusiastically.

Once in my room that Friday night, I called Peter.

He inquired, "How goes your sleuthing? Have you detected any 'bad vibes' in the Faracelli household yet?"

I scolded, "Don't make fun of me, Peter." And I said, "I feel there is something going on here, but I can't put my finger on it yet."

"How is your friend?"

"Millie is being mysterious. But that might just be her typical 'Millie' demeanor."

"How do you like her boyfriend?"

"Michael is quite appealing. I haven't talked to him much so far. He is busy getting ready for his art exhibit tomorrow."

Then he asked, "Have you met the children yet?"

"Most of them. I like Jesse. There is a nice boy hidden underneath the teenage rebellion. I talked to Gina. She doesn't seem particularly worried about her modeling career coming to an end. Tony and his wife Lisa arrived today. The striking resemblance between Tony and Anthony, his father, seems almost eerie. Guido has not made an appearance yet."

Then I said, "I miss you Peter. I wish I could take long walks with you and 'think aloud.'"

He answered, "I hope that's not the only thing you miss me for!"

"That too!"

There was a pause, and I pictured Peter smiling to himself.

Then I said, "How are you getting along?"

"So far, I can't complain."

On that note, we hung up.

Chapter 16

◇◇◇◇◇◇◇◇◇◇◇◇◇◇◇◇◇◇◇◇

Mid-morning on Saturday, we decided on the golf cart "schedule." Millie and Michael took off in the blue one ahead of everyone else. They wanted to be at the Casino Ballroom early to welcome the art critiques and enthusiasts, fellow artists, the press, as well as the general audience. Gina had offered Tony and Lisa the use of her pink cart. Lisa thought she might get tired, so this gave them the option to head home early. Jesse could not make up his mind yet whether or not he was going to attend the event at all. It was Beatrix's day off, and she had made other plans. She had left early in the morning in her yellow vehicle, presumably to take the first boat out to the mainland.

In the early afternoon, Gina and I took off down the hill in "my" red cart.

Gina commented, "You obviously enjoy driving this thing!"

"You bet!" I answered.

Then I inquired, "Do we pick up your fiancé, or will he meet us there?"

"He just called before we left. He is actually going to be delayed. He has to take care of an emergency. On Saturdays Charles shares emergency duty with another doctor, and today happens to be his turn."

"Oh, that's too bad."

Gina shrugged her shoulders and said, "That's OK. He'll be there eventually. I might as well get used to his duty calls, as a future doctor's wife."

I said, "Excellent attitude, Gina!"

The town of Avalon was crowded with "art" people, plus the usual weekend tourists. We were not the only ones headed for the Casino. Other folks flocked to the art deco palace as well. The Catalina Casino was never a gambling hall, but rather a place of gathering, dancing and festivities.

The Avalon Theatre, located at the main level, was a state-of-the-art theatre at the time of its creation in 1929. The theatre murals created by John Gabriel Beckman were spectacular. He had first designed them to be executed in glazed Catalina tile. Due to the pressures of completing the building, however, he was running out of time and the scenes were painted directly onto the concrete surface.

The nine huge panels of underwater themes against a green background at the entrance loggia were the first murals a theatergoer would see. The scene over the box office depicted underwater life centered by a mermaid. The naiad was portrayed with dramatically long, flaming hair floating in an upward sweep. The mermaid mural is now executed in tile. In 1986, artist Richard Thomas Keit in collaboration with John Gabriel Beckman redid the 10′ x 20′ art deco mermaid mural in tile.

Built above the theatre, on the top story, was the spectacular Casino Ballroom.

On entering, I was once again in awe of its elegant décor. I had seen the immense room on other visits, but it never failed to impress me. The enormous circular room had a domed umbrella ceiling, centered by a sparkling chandelier, peach-colored wall panels, and a solid parquet floor. I could picture the ballroom filled with formally attired couples, dancing to the music of big band orchestras of eras gone by.

The ballroom interior had been very cleverly set up for this occasion. Millie's sculpture placed near the entrance, titled simply "Michael," had a favorable effect. Ms Norris had known best after all! Throughout the large room, Michael's oil paintings and watercolors were ingeniously displayed, allowing enough space to show off each work to its fullest advantage.

There was a large turnout. People either stood admiring Michael's creations or gathered in little groups engaged in small talk. Millie, as well as Michael, was mixing and mingling.

Gina nudged me and said, "See that man with the cane over there? The man talking to Mom?"

Glancing in that direction, I nodded. Millie and a man that looked to be at least 85 were in deep conversation. The old man gesticulated with his cane at the painting in front of them.

Gina announced, "That's Mr. Clementine."

I looked at her dumbfounded and said, "Should I know him?"

Laughing, she replied, "I guess not. Growing up, he was a household name to us. He is an art expert, as well as Mom's personal friend. He collects art objects and is associated with several museums. He is also an art critique and occasionally promotes new, talented artists. A word of praise from him will open many doors. A long time ago, he helped Mom, when she was still struggling to get recognition."

Then she said, "Come, I'll introduce you."

As we approached, Millie and the old gentleman had just embraced and then parted.

He looked at us and exclaimed, "Ginie! What a stunning woman you've become! I still think of you as the little girl with pigtails!"

Gina said, "Great to see you, Mr. Clementine! Meet Mom's friend, Mrs. Huber."

Then she asked him, "How do you like Michael's paintings?"

He replied, "Some of them are good. Others could use improvement. On the whole, they are rather impressive.

It was definitely worth the bumpy helicopter ride over here!"

Gina beamed at him and said, "Coming from you, Mr. Clementine, that's a good critique!"

Suddenly, jumping out of nowhere it seemed, a media person shoved a microphone in the old man's face, asking, "Did I hear 'good critique,' Mr. Clementine?"

He replied, "Later, if you please. I haven't even examined all the works yet." And he moved on.

I had not noticed any cameras in the room. They must have been cleverly hidden.

Gina whispered, "I don't want them to ask me any questions about my career. I'm going outside to call Charles. See you around."

I had forgotten that she was a celebrity.

Realizing the reporter was now focusing on me, I said, "I am nobody important," and I quickly walked away from the limelight.

I enjoyed the rest of the afternoon exploring the exhibit by myself. An oil portrait in particular, titled *Grief-Stricken*, captivated me. It depicted a woman in her sixties. Her facial expression portrayed such tremendous sorrow. I felt like reaching out to her and offer my condolences.

Judging from the interest shown and the comments made by people around me, the show was a success.

As I stepped out onto the balcony, I found Jesse leaning against a pillar and looking out to the ocean.

I said, "I'm glad you decided to come."

As I came closer, I realized that he was not looking out to the ocean but rather down into the waters close by. I noticed a section of the sea marked off with buoys.

Pointing to that area, I asked, "Is this where you dive off?"

"Yes. That is the Casino Point Marine Park. I usually start my dives at the farthest buoy."

Then he said, "If you'd have gotten out here a couple of minutes earlier, you'd have seen a bunch of divers going down. I guess they're given a group lesson."

I asked, "How big is your group going to be on Monday?"

"Just my instructor and me. I take private lessons."

Then I said, "I am going back inside. Care to join me?"

He replied, "No. I'd rather stay out here a while longer. See you at dinner."

Chapter 17

◇◇◇◇◇◇◇◇◇◇◇◇◇◇◇◇◇◇◇◇

A table for dinner was reserved at a restaurant in town for friends and family, following the art exhibit. Besides the family and Pamela Norris, there were several of Millie and Michael's friends gathered around the long, rectangular table.

Ms Norris said, "Looks like we had a huge success today!"

Millie looked at Michael, saying, "It sure was! Carl Clementine liked your paintings!"

Tony said, "I talked to Mr. Clementine for quite some time. He always looked old to me, as far back as I can remember, but he must be ancient by now."

Millie agreed, "Carl is in his late eighties and I noticed that he is getting frail. His mind, however, seems to be as sharp as ever. I really appreciate his making the effort and coming to the exhibit today."

The general conversation went on along those lines, with everyone clearly pleased and excited about the outcome of the show.

Dr.Timble was seated next to me. He had a narrow face with a prominent forehead, intelligent gray eyes and a strong nose. Looking into those eyes, I felt the presence of a very strong intellect.

During the course of dinner, I addressed him, saying, "I hope your emergency was not too serious and you still had time to enjoy the event?"

He replied, "A little kid swallowed a handful of pills and we had to pump his stomach. He is OK now. The episode was a great shock to his parents and an ordeal for the child. This sort of thing happens more often than one thinks, despite the fact that every parent knows that medications should be kept locked up around little kids." Then he added, "I got to the ballroom in time to browse for almost an hour, before we came here to the restaurant."

I glanced at Millie, seated at the other end of the table. Satisfied that she was deep in conversation with Tony and Lisa, I whispered, "Speaking of pills, Doctor, would you prescribe *Sehydrin* for treating arthritis?"

He raised an eyebrow and said, "No doctor in his right mind would prescribe *Sehydrin* in the treatment of arthritis. As far as I know, the drug is not approved in the U.S. It is available in Russia, Canada, and some other countries."

And he added, "Where did you hear about *Sehydrin*?"

"Oh, I am probably confusing the name of the drug. Sorry, my mistake."

He looked at me pensively and then asked, "I understand you went to school with Mrs. Faracelli. What school was that?"

I was thinking to myself: Good for you, doctor! Check out my past. You are suspicious of a person you just met who wants to pick your brain about strange medications!

Aloud I said, "I met Mildred Faracelli and her twin sister at an international boarding school in Fribourg, Switzerland. That was over 45 years ago."

He replied, "I didn't know Mrs. Faracelli had a twin."

Gina cut in, "Of course you know, Charles. You met Aunt Lillian a week ago during her visit here."

He said, "Oh. Your Aunt Lillian is your Mom's twin sister? But they are totally different!"

"They're not identical, of course," Gina retorted.

I steered the conversation back to medicine and inquired, "Do you enjoy your work as a G.P., here on Avalon?"

He replied, "I love the island. Working as a G.P. is hopefully only temporary."

I said, "Oh yes. Gina mentioned that you are interested in doing research. Are you planning to apply to a big hospital research laboratory or to a place like UCLA?"

"No, those places are too restricted for me. I would like to open my own lab and do really interesting research, as I see fit. We've come a long way in medicine, but so many avenues in the field are still a mystery. There are countless diseases for which there are no cures to this day. I would like to work on discovering cures, not just controlling treatments, for these conditions."

While talking about his pet subject, I noticed a change in the doctor's facial expression. The normally passive, controlled poker face turned eager and enthusiastic.

I said, "That will take some capital."

He replied, "Yes. It all boils down to getting the money to start with. I've applied for loans with several banks, but they all turned me down."

I said, "I wish you the best of luck, Dr. Timble."

Gina shouted, "Oh, for Christ's sake, don't call him that! His name is Charles! So call him Charles!"

Gina's outcry was so loud and comical, everyone at the table roared with laughter.

Chuckling, I turned to the young man, and said, "What's up, Doc -- correction, Charles?"

Chapter 18

◇◇◇◇◇◇◇◇◇◇◇◇◇◇◇◇◇◇◇◇

Out on my balcony on Sunday morning, I overheard an argument in progress coming from the veranda below:

I heard Millie say, "Oh Guido! You have such a knack for business; then you go and gamble it all away! I know this current little business of yours is worthwhile, but I can't keep throwing good money after bad!"

A voice I presumed was Guido's, yelled, "What about lover boy? You have no problem supporting him and financing his art exhibits! All I need is a lousy twenty to twenty-five thousand to get me back on track!"

More was said, but they had lowered their voices and I could not hear them clearly any longer.

Later in the morning, I took a stroll on the grounds. I came across Millie up on the "lookout."

As I came up the path, she was standing at the railing, looking down to the ocean. From a distance, her flowery cotton skirt blowing slightly in the breeze, she looked like a young girl. I was strongly aware of that ageless quality about her. Coming close, I noticed that she looked tired.

At that moment she turned her head and spotted me.

She said, "I'm glad you came up here. Let's have a chat." And she led me to the wooden bench.

I asked, "Are you all right?"

"Sure."

I gave her a look that told her I knew she wasn't telling the truth.

"Reg, I'm tired. Although a great success, the art exhibit took more out of me than I realized. I'm tired of the children's problems too."

I nodded and said, "I overheard your argument with Guido, I am sorry to say."

She smiled and said, "I know. I saw your smoke signals!" And she added, "Guido has a quick temper, but his anger is usually short lived."

"I know the gist of Guido's problem from what I heard this morning. At dinner the other night, I got a glimpse of what Tony has in mind. Is there a problem concerning Gina, as well?"

"Hers is minor, compared with the boys. She just maxed out her credit cards. She is used to having the very best, so when her jobs started dwindling, her lifestyle stayed the same."

Sighing, Millie added, "I will probably give them all what they want in the end, but I'll let them stew for a while."

I said, "Have you met Beatrix's boyfriend?"

Millie answered, "No. She keeps her 'off-duty' life very private."

I commented, "Beatrix told me her boyfriend is on a safari at the moment."

"Reg! I can't believe you got any information about her private life out of her. That is amazing!"

"Well, I admit, it took some prying."

Then I said, "I understand Michael's mother lives in Southern California?"

"Yes, she does."

"Have you met?"

"No. I told Michael that I would like to meet her. Apparently she gets seasick and does not want to ride the boat to the island. I suggested that we make a trip over and visit her, but Michael seems to avoid the subject."

"Do you know why?"

She thought about it and then said, " Well, I think it could be one of two things. Michael's mother might be a simple woman, and he is ashamed of her. Another reason, which is more likely, might be that she disapproves of Michael's relationship with me."

I probed further, "Is Michael on good terms with his mother?"

"As far as I know, yes. Why do you ask?"

"Oh, I was just surprised that she was not at the art exhibit. I mean, this was a big event in her son's life."

"I hadn't thought of that. You are right, that is strange. I have to ask Michael about it. Maybe he forgot to invite her."

She got up and, limping slightly, walked back to the edge of the lookout.

I asked, "What's the matter with your leg?"

She replied, "Oh, that. I had a fall back in May and sprained my ankle. Every so often it still acts up."

"I thought you might blame it on your arthritis."

Millie ignored my remark and looked out at the ocean again, lost in her own little world, it seemed.

Then she commented, "This is my very favorite spot up here."

Suddenly she turned to me and said, "OK. Reg, what exactly are you doing here?"

Perplexed, I replied, "What do you mean?"

"Lillie hired you, didn't she?"

I admitted, "Yes, she did. I'm sorry, Millie."

Then I asked, "How did you know?"

She said, "I am aware of being 'out to lunch' most of the time, but I'm not a complete idiot. Lillie kept asking me and everyone else in the household about my fall down the stairs."

"What, exactly, made you suspect I might be here professionally?"

She smiled and said, "I first had my suspicions when Lillie called me, suggesting I should invite you. Then, when I saw you, I was sure. You didn't look overworked and tired to me. On the contrary, you seemed to be full of energy."

I laughed and said, "Who is the detective here?" Then I said, "Why didn't you say so right away?"

"Well," she said, "I knew I would enjoy your visit, Reg. I'm really glad you're here."

I inquired, "So you are not sending me packing?"

"Of course not. I get a kick out of you!"

"Now that things are out in the open, tell me all about it."

She looked puzzled and said, "Tell you about what?"

"For instance, what happened when you fell down the stairs?"

"There is nothing to tell. I fell."

I asked, "You are positive you were not pushed?"

"Yes."

I looked at her intently, not uttering a word.

She said, "Like I told Lillie and I'm telling you, I ought to know whether I fell or was pushed."

I replied, "Yes. You ought to."

Then she said, "What exactly did Lillie tell you?"

"She implied that there was something evil going on in this household, and she hired me to find out about it."

"There is nothing going on." And she added, "Where did Lillie say this 'evil' is coming from?"

I answered, "She did not know."

Millie shrugged, saying, "You'd think Lillie is the vague one! She sent you over here on a wild goose chase."

"Maybe."

"Well, Reg, feel free to snoop around, but there is nothing wrong going on in this house. In the meantime, just enjoy your vacation. I am truly happy to have you here."

"Thank you, Millie, for still making me feel welcome."

Chapter 19

◇◇◇◇◇◇◇◇◇◇◇◇◇◇◇◇◇◇◇◇

Millie had told me that on Sundays everyone just helped themselves to breakfast and lunch. I was standing at the kitchen counter, fixing myself a sandwich for a late lunch, when Guido made an appearance.

I said, "Hi, Guido. I'm Regula Huber. Can I fix you some lunch?"

He said, "Hello, Mrs. Huber. Mom told me you were visiting." And he added, "Your sandwich looks good. I'd like the same, please. Thanks!"

We carried the sandwiches and drinks out to the veranda, the outside temperature being a pleasant 86 degrees.

Sitting down and facing me across the table, Guido asked, "Where is everybody?"

I said, "Looks like everyone, besides the two of us, already had their lunch. Tony and Lisa went down to Avalon. I heard music coming from Jesse's room. I would imagine Gina is spending the day with her fiancé. Beatrix is probably still on the mainland. I understand Michael is helping Ms Norris and her team transfer his paintings back to storage. Your stepmother is very likely taking a nap."

Guido laughed, and said, "Sounds like you're keeping tabs on all the household members!"

Then he asked, "You said your first name is Regula. Are you by any chance R.A. Huber?"

Surprised, I said, "Yes. I am. What do you know about R.A. Huber?"

"I know that you are a private eye."

"Who told you?"

"Nicole Worthington."

Now I was really astonished, and I said, "You know Nicole Worthington?"

"Yes. She is one of my best customers, and I also play tennis with her."

I exclaimed, "It's a small world!"

Then I asked, "What did Nicole tell you about me?"

He grinned, and said, "Only that you are the cat's whiskers in detecting! According to her, you solved a double murder at her house."

I saw the lively, intelligent young woman clearly in my mind and inquired, "How is Nicole doing?"

He replied, "Very good. She launched a job as a scientist in the space program. I wouldn't be surprised if she'll end up as an astronaut one of these days."

We ate our lunches in silence for a while, and I had ample time to study him. There was a slight resemblance to his brother, but Guido's face was more rounded, with dimples appearing when he smiled. This gave him a mischievous, boyish look. His hair was dark like his brother's, but the eyes were blue.

I said, "From my balcony this morning, I couldn't help overhearing your fight with your stepmother."

He interrupted, "Please don't keep calling Mom my stepmother. She didn't give birth to me, but I consider her my real mom."

"All right, Guido, that is understood." And I continued, "As I said, I'm sorry I overheard your argument."

He said, "That's OK. I know I got pretty loud. I have a temper." And he added, "Mom will help me out eventually, I'm sure."

"I understand you are an entrepreneur, already on your second business."

"Yes. My first attempt at owning my own company was sort of a learning experience."

I asked, "What kind of business was it?"

He replied, "It was a beach toy store. I sold anything from children's sand toys to boogie boards, volleyball nets and sun umbrellas. I started that business straight out of college, with Mom's help, of course. I hired a salesclerk but did the rest myself. I took care of everything, from buying wholesale to keeping the books. It was a great learning experience."

I inquired, "What went wrong?"

"Oh, in the long run, I just couldn't compete with the big guys. The location was ideal, right by the beach in a little town on the mainland. But as the rent was going up, and my overhead kept increasing, big stores a few blocks away were selling the same stuff at much lower prices."

"What is your current business?" I asked.

"We sell tennis equipment: racquets, shoes and outfits, anything to do with tennis. We pride ourselves for being a small, customer-oriented business."

I said, "That sounds worthwhile. How many employees do you have on your staff?"

"There are two salespersons -- one specializing in tennis shoes, the other in racquets -- one office and computer person, one bookkeeper and one warehouse stock clerk, and myself, of course. I oversee the business, do the merchandise ordering, and am available for consultations with customers. I play and know just about anything there is to know about tennis."

I nodded approvingly, saying, "I am impressed, Guido."

After a pause, I said, "Is your mom's statement correct, that you are gambling your business away?"

He replied, "I know Mom thinks so, but that is not true. I ran into her and Michael by chance, last time I was in Vegas, and happened to be on a losing streak."

"When was that?"

"It was this June."

I said, "So the idea that you are gambling your money away was just an assumption of your mom's, and your business is doing well?"

"I didn't say that exactly. Let me explain. My business has not been doing well for the last three months. We've had a lot of unforeseen expenses. Plus the way the economy has been going, any small business is in trouble nowadays. I admit, I went to Vegas in an attempt to win some money to put into the business, but instead I was losing.

"I had no idea that Mom and Michael were in Las Vegas. Mom had apparently spotted me losing at the craps table, and then followed me to a poker game, where I lost an even bigger amount. When I looked up and saw her standing there, watching me, I nearly fainted."

I said, "I see." Then I asked, "What are you going to do if your mom does not bail you out?"

He answered, "Oh, I'm sure she will. If not, I'll have to get a loan somewhere else."

Then he winked at me, saying, "If all else fails and I lose my business, I'll just have to apply for a real job! After all, I have a business degree."

I laughed and said, "That's a good attitude!"

He gave me a scrutinizing look and then commented, "Now, Mrs. Huber, it is your turn to be honest with me. You must have a reason for looking into my financial difficulties. I can't believe that you are simply nosy. Are you here professionally?"

I nodded, "Yes, Guido, you found me out."

"It's hard for me to imagine Mom hired you."

"She didn't."

Perplexed, he asked, "Then who did?"

"I was hired by your Aunt Lillian."

After a pause, he said, "Oh, I get it. Aunt Lillian thought someone tried to murder Mom by pushing her down the stairs."

I said, "Who do you think gave her that idea?"

"I don't know. Maybe Jesse put it into her head."

"Why Jesse?"

Guido said, "The little punk tried to blackmail us."

I asked, "What do you mean by 'us'?"

"He blackmailed me, then he tried it on Gina. I would not be surprised if he had a go at Tony, as well."

"How did he blackmail you? Did he ask for money?"

"Oh no, nothing as definite as that. I think it was a game to him. He probably just wanted a reaction out of us."

"What exactly did he say?"

"Something like, 'I saw you the night Mom fell down the stairs.'"

I said, "Yes, I see." And I added, "So what was your reaction?"

Guido grinned and said, "I wanted to scare him and threatened to call the police."

Then I inquired, "What do you think? Was your mother pushed, or did she lose her footing and fall?"

"Of course she fell," he said. "The idea that one of us tried to kill her is ridiculous."

I inquired further, "I was told your mom's fall occurred in May, at her South Pasadena residence. Do you remember who was staying in her house at the time?"

"We were all there. Jesse and Beatrix live with her, of course. The rest of us were in town to celebrate Gina's birthday. We all spent the night at Mom's house, even Charles."

I said, "Was Michael Albertis there?"

"No."

I stated, "So the household consisted of the following people that night: your mom, Jesse, Beatrix, Tony, Lisa, Gina, Charles and yourself. Correct?"

"Yes." And he added, "None of us would want to harm Mom. We all love her."

"It seems that way," I said.

Chapter 20

◇◇◇◇◇◇◇◇◇◇◇◇◇◇◇◇◇◇◇◇

Lisa joined us on the veranda. Flopping herself into a chair, she said, "I'm bushed."

I asked, "Did you and Tony enjoy yourselves in Avalon?"

"Yes. It was fun. I did a little shopping, but we mostly just walked around. Tony is checking out the *Airport-In-The-Sky,* as we speak. We ran into Beatrix and she kindly gave me a ride home."

Guido said, "If you'll excuse me, I'll go hit the little town myself." And winking at me, he added, "Who knows, I might even find a little poker game!"

Beatrix, who had come out behind Lisa, said, "You can take the yellow cart. I don't need it anymore today."

Guido said, "Thanks, Beatrix." And waving to us all, he disappeared.

Lisa looked shocked and said, "I didn't know there was gambling allowed on Catalina Island."

I said, "Of course there aren't any poker games to be had in Avalon. Guido was just having his little joke with me."

Beatrix, obviously back from the mainland, had brought the pitcher of lemonade out, refilled my drink, and set a glass of iced water in front of Lisa. That woman was a wizard!

I turned to Lisa and said, "This is like being in your favorite restaurant, where the waitress knows what you want before you give your order!"

Lisa replied, "Beatrix is the greatest!"

Then I asked, "How are you feeling?"

"Pregnant women are supposed to have a 'special glow.' All I feel is tired and apprehensive."

"Are you worried about the future?"

"Yes. When Tony and I decided it was time to start a family, both of us had jobs. Now we have no income. Tony was laid off, and I had to quit."

I asked, "How long has Tony been laid off?"

"Since March. We've been living from our savings, but they are dwindling rapidly. I worked until the beginning of May."

"What is your profession?"

"I'm a flight attendant."

Then I asked, "Do you think it a good idea for Tony to start his airline business?"

She replied, "I support him, of course, but I'm worried that it won't be as easy as he thinks. He is a terrific pilot, but it will be a great risk to take on. He'll need a lot of money to start with. He'll have to purchase an airplane, and there are tons of expenses besides that. If he succeeds with starting the business, then it will cost a lot to keep it going."

I remarked, "I understand he wants his mom to invest in the venture."

"Yes. That is basically why we are here this time. He is so enthusiastic about his plan and feels it will be a great success, that he has no doubt he can convince Mildred to make the investment."

I said, "Well, I wish you and Tony the best of luck." Then I asked, "Is Tony's venture your only anxiety?"

She looked at me hesitantly and then said, "Well, I have other worries too."

"Having to do with the baby?"

"Yes. I'm worried that I might not make a good mother."

"Oh, Lisa. Every woman has the potential to become a good mother. It is simply instinct. The only ones that make bad parents are selfish people. You don't strike me as being selfish."

At that moment a transforming smile came over her, and she said, "He's kicking!"

I replied, "See, the baby agrees!"

Tony joined us later that afternoon.

He looked at Lisa and said, "You are positively glowing, Honey!" Turning to me, he said, "Do you know where Mom is, Mrs. Huber? I can't wait to talk to her about my plans."

I replied, "I think she is taking a nap." Then I said, "I understand you want to start your own business. What kind of flight company do you have in mind?"

He explained, "Scheduled flights to and from Catalina. It's really a great idea, you know. At the moment there are no scheduled flights to Avalon, only a helicopter service. There is a landing strip called *The-Airport-In-The-Sky*, located in the island's interior, about ten miles from Avalon. At present it is only used for private planes and maybe UPS. I've checked it out."

I commented, "I can imagine that starting a flight business of that sort would be very involved?"

"Somewhat. I'll need permits and licenses and, of course, a plane to start out with."

"Of course!"

He continued, "I've looked into buying an aircraft. There are some older model Cessnas available, in good condition and quite reasonable."

"What is reasonable for a plane?"

"About $900,000 to one and a half million."

I raised my eyebrows, saying, "Sorry for being so blunt, but I think you expect a lot from your stepmother."

He replied, "My what? Oh, of course. I forgot Mom is not my real mother. Anyhow, I don't expect her to buy me an aircraft, just loan me the money for a down payment."

"I see."

"I wouldn't be averse to Mom's becoming a partner in the business, if she prefers to make her investment in that way."

Smiling, I commented, "You are giving her two different options, in other words."

"Are you making fun of me, Mrs. Huber?"

"Maybe just a little," I said.

Chapter 21

◇◇◇◇◇◇◇◇◇◇◇◇◇◇◇◇◇◇◇

The next morning, Monday, I ventured down to Avalon for a little jog. This time my run took me along the major street leading away from the harbor. I passed the Sheriff's Station, then the Municipal Hospital, which was a small one-story building. I remembered being told on a previous visit to the island, that this was only a 12-bed hospital. As I passed the public school, I slowed my jog to a fast walk, the terrain leading slightly uphill. A little farther I came upon a golf course to my right, and to the left I was looking at the Catalina riding stables.

Heading towards a baseball field, I was thinking, this must be the field where William Wrigley, Jr. took his Chicago Cubs for their spring practice for many years! Then I came upon a sign, *To Wrigley Memorial & Botanical Garden*. I opted not to hike up the hill to it and turned around.

I was done with my exercising for the day and was just within a few yards of where my golf cart was parked when I noticed Jesse drive by in his green cart. He waved, and I realized he was on the way to his diving instruction. I changed my mind about heading home to the Faracelli house and followed Jesse to the Casino Point Marine Park instead. We both parked our vehicles behind the casino building.

Jesse walked towards me saying, "What's up?"

I replied, "I hope you don't mind if I watch you getting ready for your dive?"

He said, "OK with me," as he hauled his equipment off the golf cart.

"Remember, you were going to share some of your diving experience with me," I said.

He nodded and asked, "What do you want to know?"

"For starters," I said, "Why don't you explain your equipment to me as you don each piece."

"Sure," he said, and started his demonstration. "First I strap the buoyancy control device onto the tank." Then he explained, "Now I'm attaching the regulator, the alternate air source, and dive computer to the tank."

As he did this, I noticed that hoses linked these items.

He continued, "Now I make sure I have enough air in my tank," and he turned the valve on.

Surveying his dive computer, he stated, "Good, I have 3000 psi."

I inquired, "What does 'psi' stand for?"

"Pounds per square inch."

"Are there other functions to your computer, besides checking the psi?"

Jesse replied, "Yes. Under water I check the depth, air pressure and time." Then he said, "So the tank stuff is ready, and now I'll put my gear on."

I had noticed that a little distance away, a young man I took to be the instructor was checking his own equipment and was donning his gear.

As Jesse was ready to put on his suit, I asked, "Are there different types of diving suits?"

"Yes. This is a wetsuit, which is perfectly fine for summers in California. They are made of a material called Neoprene. It does not keep you dry, since water gets underneath the suit. After I'm certified, I'll buy a dry-suit, which keeps you dry and warm, since I'm planning to dive year round."

He struggled into his wetsuit, the garment being so tight he had to wriggle into it, limb by limb. Then Jesse donned his boots, his gloves and some type of belt around his waist.

Pointing at the latter, I asked, "What is that for?"

"That's a weight belt with weights," and clearly enjoying sharing his knowledge, he lectured on the subject. "When I wear this 7mm-thick wetsuit, I also need a weight belt to compensate for the buoyancy of the wetsuit. With the correct amount of weight, I would slowly sink. To avoid this, I wear a buoyancy control device, simply called BCD by divers. With the attached power inflator to the BCD, I inflate the BCD by pressing the power inflate button. This will make me float. In order to descend, I must empty the inflated BCD by holding the power inflator up and dumping air by pressing the dump valve."

Next Jesse shouldered the tank with the BCD, which he wore like a backpack, and grabbed his mask with snorkel and his fins.

At that moment the instructor walked towards us and said, "Ready, Jesse?"

"You bet!" said Jesse, and the two walked to the stairs leading into the water. Arriving at the bottom step, they slipped into their fins. Then I watched them float on their backs toward the farthest buoy. Once there, just as Jesse had explained, I saw them raise their power inflators and dump air. They slowly descended and were out of my sight.

Chapter 22

Back at the Faracelli residence I quickly showered and determined some leisure time was in order for the remainder of the morning. I took a book to the lookout and settled in on the bench. As usual, I found myself surrounded by peace and tranquility up there. There was something deeply relaxing, looking down to the vast waters of the ocean. No wonder this was Millie's favorite hangout. It had become my preferred spot as well.

Deeply involved in my book, I was unaware of a girl's approach until she stood next to the bench. She looked to be about twelve years old, was skinny, had medium brown hair hanging loosely down her back, intelligent gray eyes, and a general air of "matter of fact" about her.

She said, "Sorry to interrupt. Have you seen Jesse around?"

I smiled and said, "Hi. You sneaked up on me! Where did you come from so suddenly?"

She replied, "Oh, sorry. I'm Julia Jacobs. I live over there," and she pointed to the house beyond the tall hedge separating the two properties.

She added, "You must be Mrs. Faracelli's friend. Jesse told me about you."

I said, "Yes. I am she. My name is Regula Huber." Then I said, "Coming back to your question, Jesse is having a diving lesson this morning."

"Oh, I know. He is supposed to come play with me in the treehouse after his lesson. What time is it?"

I looked at my watch, saying, "10:25."

She nodded, "He should be here soon, then."

"Are you Jesse's friend?"

"Yes, here on the island. He probably wouldn't acknowledge me at his school or anywhere else. I'm just a little kid to him."

"How old are you, Julia?"

"Fourteen." And she added, "I don't have any sex appeal yet, but I'm working on it. People of your generation call me 'a late bloomer,' I suppose."

Laughing, I said, "Full bloom is just around the corner!" Then I asked, "What do you and Jesse play in the treehouse?"

"We have all sorts of games up there. Chess, checkers, cards, backgammon, Trivial Pursuit, and more."

"What fun!" I exclaimed.

Then I inquired, "How long have you known Jesse?"

She replied, "Three years. We only see each other in summer, though."

"Do you live on the mainland and vacation here in the summer?"

"My mother lives in Arizona, and my father lives here all year round. They're divorced. I stay with Mom during the school year and with Dad in the summer."

"I see."

"Dad is a writer, so he can live anywhere he wants. He does not have to worry about any commute to and from work."

I commented, "My husband is a writer also."

She said, "Are you still married?"

Bemused, I replied, "Very much so."

"Do you find him hard to live with?"

Puzzled with this question, I said, "Not particularly."

Julia stated, "You are lucky. Mom told me it is impossible to live with a writer."

I said, "My husband only became a writer after he retired. It is more like a hobby with him."

She said, "Well, that's different." Then she asked, "Are you retired too?"

"Yes. But I keep myself occupied as well. I started my own little business, since my retirement."

"What kind of business?"

"I own a detective agency."

She blurted out, "Oh! How thrilling!" And scrutinizing me from head to toe, she said, "Yes. I can picture you as a private eye."

After a long pause, she said, "Are you here incognito?"

Chuckling, I replied, "I was. But I've been found out."

"Whom are you investigating? Or am I not allowed to know?"

I answered, "It's not 'whom' but rather 'what.'" And I added, "I don't mind telling you. Possibly, you have already heard about it. I am looking into the fall Mrs. Faracelli had down her stairs last May."

Julia said, "Yes. Jesse told me about it."

"What did he tell you?"

"Oh, just that there was talk his mom might have been pushed."

"Does Jesse think she was pushed?"

"No. He thinks she fell by herself."

"Do you have an opinion on this, Julia?"

"I don't know. It seems hard to imagine that anyone would want to harm Mrs. Faracelli."

"I agree."

Changing the subject, I said, "I take it you know that Jesse has been in trouble this last school year?"

She nodded, "You mean the drugs. Yes, I know about that. He has shaped up, though. Apparently he got himself mixed up with the wrong crowd during his junior year. He wants to have nothing to do with those guys anymore now."

"Good!"

She continued, "You've got to understand. Jesse is very sensitive. He felt extremely rejected when his father skipped town without a word. Ever since I've known him, he has struggled with living that down. Then add the normal rebellion teenagers have against authority and their parents, and someone like Jesse gets easily swayed by peer pressure."

I said, "Have you given any thought to becoming a psychiatrist, Julia?"

She just shrugged her shoulders.

Then I said, "His mom seems to be understanding and has helped him back on track. I'm thinking of the fact that she hired a tutor to catch him up with his school work, as well as getting him involved with diving lessons, which he seems to enjoy."

Julia agreed, "Jesse has always appreciated and loved his mom, even if he didn't show it with his actions. He needs a lot of attention, and Mrs. Faracelli has been preoccupied with her boyfriend lately. The diving instructions have transformed Jesse most of all. He loves to dive."

I inquired, "What do you think of Mrs. Faracelli? Do you like her?"

She answered, "She is a very kind lady. I like her, but she can be spooky, sometimes."

"What do you mean by 'spooky?'"

"Well, she has this way of staring into space. One gets the feeling she is far away and might never return. It totally spooks me out."

"Yes. I've experienced that with her too, once or twice."

I surveyed her for a minute and then said, "Let me tell you what I think of you, Julia Jacobs: You might be a late bloomer, but you are wise way beyond your years!"

At that moment we heard footsteps sounding from the stepping-stones leading up to our ledge, followed by Jesse's appearance.

I said, "Here he comes!" And once he was close to us, I added, "How was your dive?"

"Awesome, simply awesome! I had a tug-a-war with an octopus!"

I turned to Julia, saying, "I know the two of you are planning to play games, but can I borrow Jesse for a little while first? I promise I won't keep him long, but I need to ask him a few questions."

She replied, "No problem." And to Jesse she commented, "Just give me a whistle, once you're up in the treehouse."

Chapter 23

◇◇◇◇◇◇◇◇◇◇◇◇◇◇◇◇◇◇◇◇

I watched Julia walk in the direction of the hedge, and I asked Jesse, "Doesn't she have to go around and up to the street in order to reach her house? When I explored the grounds the other day, I did not notice any access between the two properties."

He replied, "You are right, there isn't any. Years ago, Julia and I discovered a little clearing in the hedge further down, and we manage to squeeze through. It is getting harder for me now, since I've grown bigger."

I commented, "I had a nice chat with Julia. You've got a very good friend here."

He said, "Julia is OK. She's a little kid, of course, but she is good company."

Then I said, "All right, Jesse. I am going to be honest with you. Did you know that I am a detective?"

He looked at me, surprised, and said, "No." And he added, "No offense, but I thought policewomen retired much earlier."

"I'm not from the police. I am a private detective."

"Oh, I see. Mom told me that you had a business and needed a rest, but she did not tell me what kind of business."

"I am here on a job, Jesse."

"Are you working on a heist or something down in Avalon, and you're staying with us, sort of under cover?"

"No. I am looking into something here, in this household."

Jesse's eyes got big, and he said, "I don't understand. I've totally shaped up. I've had nothing to do with drugs in months. How could Mom think such a thing and hire you?"

I assured him, "It has nothing to do with drugs. I am looking into that fall down the stairs your mother had in May."

"Mom hired you to look into that?" he said, surprised.

"I was hired by your Aunt Lillian."

"Oh."

I said, "Jesse, blackmail is a very serious matter. It is not a game"

"I know."

"You don't seem to understand how serious, or you would not have made an attempt at it."

Jesse looked at me, perplexed, and asked, "Who said I blackmailed anyone?"

"Guido claims you blackmailed him after your mom's fall."

"Oh, that. After there was all the talk about her maybe having been pushed, I just wanted to see every one's reaction, and I pretended I knew something. I did not ask for any money, or favors, or anything. So how can that be blackmail?"

I said, "For the person, or persons, you hinted to that you either saw or knew something about your mother's fall, it certainly sounded like blackmail. Legally, it definitely would be considered blackmail."

He looked scared now and said, "Are you going to report me?"

I said, "No, Jesse, but I want the absolute truth from you. Is that understood?"

"Yes."

"Who else did you blackmail?"

He replied, "You already know about Guido. I also tried it on Gina, Tony and Beatrix."

I shook my head and said, "Jesse, do you have any idea at all how dangerous that was for you?"

"No. Nobody seemed to take me seriously anyhow."

I said, "So you blackmailed the people you just mentioned, to get a reaction out of them. What exactly was each person's reaction?"

Jesse answered, "Guido threatened to call the police. Gina just laughed at me. Beatrix threatened to beat me up. I didn't get a reaction from Tony at all. He either didn't hear what I said or he just ignored me."

"Promise me, Jesse, that you'll never, ever blackmail anyone again."

Close to tears now, he said, "I promise."

Then I asked, "From whom did you first learn that there was a question about whether your mom was pushed or fell down the stairs on her own?"

"I don't remember. Probably from Aunt Lillian."

I said, "In your opinion, did your mom fall or was she pushed?"

He replied, "She fell."

"How do you know?"

"She said so."

"That simple!" I stated. Then I smiled at him and said, "Let's talk about a more pleasant subject. Please continue with enlightening me about your scuba diving. Let's see, where did we leave off at the Casino Point Marine Park earlier this morning?"

Jesse looked at me in amazement, saying, "You still want to know more? Now that I know you're a sleuth on a job here, I thought you just pretended to be interested."

"Oh no. Being a detective does not mean I have no other interests. I enjoy a private life as well. I would love to get further informed about diving."

Jesse's whole face lit up, and he said, "What do you want to know?"

I said, "First tell me about your encounter with the octopus today."

"That was totally awesome! I shined my flashlight into a hole, and this octopus grabbed it with his tentacles. I tried to pull the flashlight back, but the little devil wouldn't let go. We played tug-a-war with each other for the longest time. I was surprised how strong the little critter was. We had a lot of fun together, that octopus and I. You'd have had to be there to appreciate the whole thing."

I said, "I'll take your word for it, Jesse. I'm slightly claustrophobic, and I doubt whether I would have the courage to go down there."

"Oh, you wouldn't pass the medical anyhow. Before anyone can start taking scuba diving instructions, they have to pass a physical. There is a long questionnaire the doctor has to fill out and sign, to prove you are in top shape. No heart, lung, respiratory problems; no history of epilepsy or other seizures, et cetera. The list of 'no' conditions is very long. You look in good shape, but at your age, there's bound to be something wrong with you."

I laughed, saying, "Yes. There is bound to be!"

Then he said, eagerly, "What else do you want to know?"

"Oh, lots of things. Let's start with the mechanics. You told me that you take private lessons to get your scuba certification. How often is that?"

"Usually twice a week, Mondays and Wednesdays. This week I'm only getting one, today's, since my instructor has to go off the island and won't be here on Wednesday." Clearly excited, he added, "I'll be getting my open water certification after my last lesson, next Monday!"

I asked, "On your first lesson, did the instructor take you straight down?"

He replied, "Oh no. First I had to take theory, and then I had some pool practices before I was taken out on the ocean."

"Is there a special breathing technique you are using under water?"

He replied, "You breathe slower and deeper than normal, with slow inhalations and exhalations."

"Do you always dive off the Casino Point Marine Park, or do you sometimes dive off a boat?"

"Yes, I asked the instructor once to take me out on a boat. We motored to a different part of the island, where we found a great cove with the coolest kelp forest."

I inquired further, "Once you are certified, will you be able to dive by yourself?"

He replied, "Without an instructor, but never alone. Diving alone would be very dangerous. There should be at least two divers. It's called the buddy system. That way, if something should go wrong with your equipment, there is another person to help you out."

"Do you communicate with your buddy under water?"

"Yes. We use sign language."

Then I said, "When you showed me your equipment earlier, I didn't notice a flashlight, yet you carried one today. Did you just forget to show it to me, or is it not essential?"

He said, "A flashlight is not needed for safety, but I carry one. It comes in handy to find eels and lobsters hiding in rocks and holes."

"And don't forget octopuses," I said. "What else do you see down there?"

Smiling, he replied, "Giant sea fans, who look like plants, but actually are animals. Calico bass, patched olive green, brown and white. Sheapheads and schools of blacksmith. If I'm lucky, I spot eels and bat rays, which are stingrays that look like underwater bats. Catalina is known for its kelp forests and garibaldi, a bright orange fish. This fish is very curious and comes close to divers."

Jesse enthusiastically went on, "Diving through the giant kelp is like swimming through a forest. There is always just a little bit of surge which makes the giant kelp move from side to side. When the sun is out, the rays dance through the kelp stalks.

"There is also a plaque dedicated to *Jacques Cousteau* and a couple of sunken sailboats down there."

I asked, "How long can you stay down with one tank, before you run out of air?"

"It depends on the depth, but usually about 45 minutes to one hour," he answered.

Then I said, "Well, Jesse, I have learned a lot and enjoyed finding out about your adventures under water. Thank you for sharing so much." And I added, "I'm afraid I've kept you too long. Julia must be getting impatient."

He grinned at me and was gone.

Chapter 24

◇◇◇◇◇◇◇◇◇◇◇◇◇◇◇◇◇◇◇

On my way back to the house, I spotted Beatrix in the rose garden. She was carefully cutting the dead flowers off each rose bush. I strolled down the stepping-stones towards her and, as I got closer, noticed that she expertly clipped the stems at a slanted angle, making sure she cut exactly above the five-leaf branches.

I commented, "I can see you are an expert with roses. Is there anything in house or garden you are ignorant about?"

She laughed, and answered, "Plenty, I'm afraid."

Then she inquired, "Are you still enjoying your visit here, or are you starting to get bored?"

"Not at all. I took a book up to the lookout, but had unexpected company before I finished the first chapter."

"Oh?"

I said, "A very interesting young lady named Julia Jacobs kept me entertained."

Beatrix nodded, "Yes, I've noticed that kid is extremely sharp."

"Later, Jesse came up and told me all there is to know about scuba diving. Earlier today, he showed me his equipment at the Casino Point Marine Park. I was fascinated! I had no idea there was so much gear and knowledge involved in the sport."

She said, "Kind of scary down there, I would imagine."

I replied, "Scary to us, but absolutely *awesome* to Jesse!"

Then I said, "We also talked about something else." And eyeing her keenly, I continued, "I understand Jesse tried to blackmail you."

She stared and then said, "Blackmail me?"

"After my friend's fall down her stairs."

"Oh, that."

"According to Jesse, you threatened to beat him up in reaction to his attempted blackmail."

Irate, she protested, "I did no such thing!" Then she thought about it and said, "Oh. I remember now. I told him: 'What you need is a good spanking.'"

"I see."

I probed further, "What do you think happened to Mildred Faracelli on those stairs?"

Beatrix answered, "She lost her footing and fell."

"You don't think she could have been pushed?"

"In theory, she could have been, but I think that's rubbish. Who would want to push her?"

I said, "Who indeed?" Then I asked, "Where is Millie? I haven't seen her yet today."

She replied, "Mrs. Faracelli is working in her studio."

"I don't want to disturb her, then. Do you think it is OK if I use her golf cart this afternoon?"

"Oh, surely. She doesn't need it today."

"Thanks, Beatrix." And I added, "I won't be here for lunch. I'm going to explore the town some more."

That said, I left the good housekeeper.

Chapter 25

◇◇◇◇◇◇◇◇◇◇◇◇◇◇◇◇◇◇◇

After changing into a cotton summer dress and sandals, I took off down the hill for the second time that Monday.

Avalon looked quiet and peaceful again, with the weekend crowd gone. Some vacationing tourists remained, and the locals ran their errands. I strolled to the Casino and back first, admiring the beautiful tile murals along the walkway. Then I ventured onto the Green Pleasure Pier, surveying the harbor around me. I passed the chamber of commerce and visitors bureau. The tourist attractions were tempting: rental of boats, jet skis, and tours on the submarine or glass bottom boats, and the nighttime flying fish excursions. I had done most of these on previous visits, so I left the pier and headed for the little shops and boutiques on the main drag of the town.

Following the purchases of a couple of presents for my grandchildren and a chic straw hat for myself, I was ready for lunch.

Waiting to get seated, I was surprised by Charles coming up to me, saying, "Come sit with us." And he led me to a table where Gina sat.

I said, "Oh, but I don't want to intrude on you young people."

Gina replied, "Don't be silly, you're not intruding." And looking at the packages I carried, she added, "I see you've enjoyed yourself!"

"You bet! I would have shopped even longer, but I got hungry." And I added, "What a pleasant surprise to run into you!"

Gina said, "We're used to running into family and friends here. It's such a small town; you're bound to come across people you know all the time. So we constantly have to be on our best behavior!"

As the waitress appeared, Charles said to me, "We've already ordered. I recommend the chicken salad."

"Chicken salad, it is," I said.

Then Gina commented, "Before you joined us, we were discussing our wedding plans. We both agree that we want to get married on Catalina. But we have a difference of opinion as to the type of ceremony and the amount of people we want to share the event with. Charles wants to keep it very small and simple, with ceremony and reception in a restaurant, and only family and a handful of close friends invited. I, on the other hand, want a big formal wedding ceremony in church, with at least four bridesmaids and two hundred guests. My idea of the reception is a gala affair in the Casino Ballroom, live band and all."

Then she grinned and said, "We want to keep this democratic. So far, the votes are one to one. We need your input, Mrs. Huber, as the deciding vote!"

I smiled and responded, "You seem to forget something. I am from Switzerland and therefore neutral!"

We all burst out laughing.

The meal concluded, Charles excused himself and said, "I enjoyed my lunch break, but it's time to get to my practice. The first afternoon patient is probably already waiting for me."

He kissed Gina, waved to me, and quickly made his exit.

Gina sighed and said, "He has a brilliant mind, you know. I feel he's wasting his genius as a G.P."

I replied, "Yes. I can see that."

She continued, "He doesn't talk about it much, but I know he's frustrated. He wants to start his lab, and all his loan applications have been turned down."

"Have you thought about asking your mom for a loan?"

"Of course I have. Charles is too proud and won't allow me to ask her."

I said, "I like that about him."

"Well, I think it's silly of him," she said.

After a pause, I commented, "I assume there will be a big inheritance for you, someday."

She replied, "Yes, but Charles can't wait that long."

When I tried to pay for our lunches, the waitress said it had already been taken care of. Charles must have paid on his way out.

Once outside, I asked, "What are your plans for the rest of the afternoon?"

"I'm free as a bird," she replied.

"I noticed a miniature golf course close by this morning. Do you feel like playing?"

"Sure."

The 18-hole miniature course turned out to be pretty unusual and quite challenging. We had a great time. I ended up the winner, but the scores were close.

Gina said, "You are pretty good. Do you play a lot?"

"Actually, very seldom. It was pure luck."

As we were walking away from the miniature golf, Gina asked, "Do you play the real thing?"

"If you mean golf, yes, I do."

"There is a golf course here on the island. It is rather unique since its nine holes have two tees each, so it can be played as an 18-hole course."

I said, "That must be the course I noticed on my jog this morning." And I added, "I don't take golfing all that seriously. Besides, I did not bring my clubs on this trip."

We had arrived at the main drag of Avalon where our carts were parked.

Pointing ahead, I said, "Look, we are not the only ones in town."

Beatrix was busily loading groceries onto her cart and, seeing us, she waved. Then we caravanned up the hill towards home. Our rooftops would have posed a colorful picture of yellow, pink and red from an aerial shot above.

Chapter 26

◇◇◇◇◇◇◇◇◇◇◇◇◇◇◇◇◇◇◇

On Tuesday, Millie had some business to attend to on the mainland. I volunteered to take her down to the docks early in the morning since I had planned to go for another jog.

Driving down the hill, Millie suddenly shouted, "Reg, control yourself. The speed limit is 20 mph!"

I said, "Sorry, I get carried away. Riding this thing is so much fun!"

We had to wait about 15 minutes before Millie could board, so we sat down on a bench.

I asked, "What kind of errands are you planning to run today? Or is it presumptuous of me to ask?"

She replied, "Oh, nothing mysterious. I have a doctor's appointment and some legal business I have to take care of. Both are in Pasadena, so I should be back by late afternoon or early evening."

"Are you sick?"

She looked at me, astonished, and then she said, "Oh, you mean the doctor's appointment. It's just a check-up."

I asked, "How do you get from Long Beach to Pasadena?"

"I've ordered a limo service. They'll pick me up and bring me back."

I said, "Call me when you've returned, and I'll come get you."

"Actually, Michael will do that. We have a dinner date in town."

"That sounds romantic!"

"I'm sure it will be!"

When it was time for her to board, I suddenly embraced her affectionately, saying, "Good bye, Millie, take care."

She looked at me, surprised, and laughingly said, "I'm only gone for the day, Reg. You act as if I'm leaving on a trip around the world!" Then she waved and stepped onto the boat.

I don't know what had possessed me to become so emotional with Millie. During my jogging routine, I was able to shake off my worries and fears. I concentrated on my pace and my breathing. By the time I had stopped running, I was back to my normal self.

Besides my other essentials, I had also managed to squeeze my cell phone into the fanny pack. It was time to make a few calls.

First I dialed a Las Vegas number to a fellow private eye. We help each other out, now and then.

"Hi Burt! R.A. Huber here. How are you?"

"Hot! Temperatures have been in the three-digit range for weeks! How are things in Pasadena?"

I replied, "I'm on Catalina at the moment."

He said, "How nice for you! Are you just there for the day?"

"I've been here since last Wednesday. I'm on a case."

"I'm jealous. I wish someone would send me to Catalina!" Then he asked, "What can I do for you?"

I said, "I would like you to check something for me in Vegas," and I told him what I wanted to know.

"Sure, no problem. I'll get back to you."

My next call was to Boston. Lillie picked up herself, which was surprising.

I said, "Hi, Lillie. I expected your secretary to answer."

She replied, "I'm in a taxi. I have my office calls switched to my cell phone."

"Oh, I don't want to intrude on you."

"You're not intruding. I'm on my way to a lunch meeting with some pharmaceutical big shots. It's clear across town, so I have plenty of time to talk to you. Did you find anything out, Reg?"

I said, "Lunch already? Of course, you are three hours ahead of us. I don't have much to report yet. I agree with you, not everything is what it seems in the Faracelli household. I have some ideas of what could be going on, but it is all theory. Nothing concrete yet."

Lillie said, "But you feel the bad vibes, the way I did?"

I replied, "I feel something odd is going on." And I added, "By the way, I was found out, but Millie did not send me packing."

"Oh, she wouldn't."

Then I said, "I have a few questions, Lillie."

"Shoot."

"Do you know the name of Millie's doctor?"

"Let me think. I should know his name. Millie sent me to him last December, when I was in California and had a bad earache during the holidays. He had a funny name too. It will come to me in a minute. Why do you want to know?"

I said, "Oh, just an idea of mine, which I'd like to check out."

She replied, "I'm sure Beatrix would know."

"I don't want to ask anyone in the household. Don't worry about it, Lillie." And I said, "I have more questions. Do you know of any lawyers Millie deals with?"

Lillie said, "The estate lawyers she uses are the offices of Samuelson, Rosenbaum & Blight. I don't know of any others she might be dealing with." And she asked, "What's this about?"

I explained, "I just dropped Millie off at the docks. She has business to tend to on the mainland, a doctor's appointment and some legal matter. Do you happen to know if she's involved in a lawsuit?"

"I don't know. I doubt it."

Then I asked, "Do you know where Samuelson, Rosenbaum & Blight are located?"

She answered, "I happen to know them myself. They're in Pasadena."

"You actually know them? That is great. Maybe you can open their door for me."

"Reg, I have no idea what you are talking about!"

"Well, you know how tight lawyers are. They probably won't tell me anything unless I show some clout. How well do you know them, Lillie?"

She laughed, and said, "You're in luck. Both Millie and I know them well. They are an old established law firm, and Father already used them as his estate attorneys. The old guys are gone, of course, but their sons took over. I usually deal with Samuelson, and I think Millie does too."

I said, "Fantastic! Can you call Mr. Samuelson and put a good word in for me?"

She replied, "You're not going to tell me what you have in mind?"

"Not yet."

"OK. Reg. I'll call him. I don't have his number with me. I'll get it from my secretary as soon as we hang up."

I said, "I appreciate it."

She suddenly exclaimed, "I have it! It's Frizzi!"

"What?"

"Millie's doctor. I just thought of his name. Frizzi, spelled F-r-i-z-z-i."

"Wonderful!" I added, "One more thing. I know you don't have it with you, but I would like Mrs. Albertis's address, when you get a chance."

She said, "Who is Mrs. Albertis?"

I replied, "Michael's mother."

"Oh, of course. I'll find it for you. I have it at home in the report on Michael's background check."

Then she said, "Anything else?"

"No. That'll do it."

"I'll call Mr. Samuelson within the next hour or so." And she commented, "I have no clue where you are going with all this, but you are the sleuth!"

I said, "Thanks a million!"

My last call was to Peter.

I said, "Do me a favor and look up a couple of numbers in the Pasadena phone book. One is a Dr. Frizzi. I have no first name. The other is the Law Offices of Samuelson, Rosenbaum & Blight."

Peter said, "You're already dealing with doctors and lawyers. You must be making progress!"

I replied, "I had a couple of brainstorms which I'm trying to follow up on, but I'm nowhere near seeing my way clearly."

Then I inquired, "How are things on the home front?"

"Tough!"

"Oh?"

"People think we are close to getting a divorce."

I asked, "What people?"

He explained, "Our 'Sunshine' called. I thought I played it smart by not telling her you were on a case. Remember the time you investigated the Worthington murder case and she read me the Riot Act about it for ten minutes?"

"How could I forget?"

Peter continued, "Anyhow, when she phoned, I told her that you needed a break and are vacationing at your friend's house on Catalina Island. She then asked me when I expected you back. When I told her I had no idea, she said, 'Oh Dad! I am so sorry you and Mom are having marital problems. If you want to talk, I'm here for you.'"

"Oh brother!"

Then I asked, "Who else?"

"Maurice at *Chez Tante Jeanne*. When I showed up by myself for the second time in the same week, he raised his eyebrows, gave me a knowing, disapproving look, saying 'Table for one again?'"

I laughed and said, "I guess I'll have to set Maurice straight, once back in town!"

Peter promised he would call me back with the phone numbers, and we ended the call.

Chapter 27

◇◇◇◇◇◇◇◇◇◇◇◇◇◇◇◇◇◇◇◇

I was sitting in one of the wicker chairs on my balcony that Tuesday afternoon, when Peter called me back with the two numbers. There was only one Dr. Frizzi listed in the Pasadena book, the first name being George.

Burt from Las Vegas also called with the information I had requested.

I said, "Thanks, Burt, I owe you one."

He joked, "How about adding me to your staff on Catalina Island?"

"If I need any extra muscle, I'll let you know!"

I went into my room to make the calls, not wanting to take the chance of being overheard out on the balcony. I called Dr. George Frizzi's office.

I reached the receptionist and said, "This is Beatrix Primrose, Mrs. Faracelli's housekeeper. I hope Mrs. Faracelli is still at your office. It is very important that I talk to her."

"Just a moment, please."

Coming back on the line, she said, "Mrs. Faracelli is not here. She did not have an appointment with us today."

I said, "That's impossible. Mrs. Faracelli told me this morning that she was going to the mainland to see her doctor. There is an emergency here at her house, and I need to reach her right away."

"Hold on, please."

The woman got back to me, and said, "You might try Dr. Hugo Tobleron. We referred Mrs. Faracelli to him a while back."

I said, "OK, I'll try his office. I have his number. Hopefully she is still there. Thanks."

I thought to myself: Well, that was easy! Now all I have to find out is what this Dr. Tobleron specializes in. I reflected for a moment and quickly came up with a plan. Then I called Pasadena information and got a Dr. Hugo Tobleron's number.

"Dr. Tobleron's office. How can I help you?"

"Hello. My name is Sandy Waters. I would like to make an appointment with Dr. Tobleron."

"Who is your referral, please?"

I said, "My referral?"

"Yes. The doctor who referred you to us."

"I don't have one."

She said, "I'm sorry. Dr. Tobleron only sees patients with referrals from other doctors."

I asked, "Can't I just schedule a physical with Dr. Tobleron?"

"You want a general physical?"

"Yes."

"You need to find a G.P. or an internal medicine physician."

"Isn't that what Dr. Tobleron is?"

By this time she sounded annoyed, and said, "No. Dr. Tobleron is an oncologist and neurologist."

I said, "Oh. Sorry," and hung up.

I thought, Bingo!

It was too early to call the law firm. I wanted to give Millie time to have her business with the lawyers over and done with by the time I made my call. If indeed she was going to see Samuelson, Rosenbaum & Blight, that was.

I felt antsy, and since I couldn't think of anything better to do, I went for a walk on the Faracelli property. I took the same route as on the first day I had explored the grounds, taking the lower path which led underneath the overhanging ledge, now known to me as the lookout. I heard the echo of my footsteps again as I walked along the undercut. Still apprehensive about Millie, the echo sent shivers up my spine.

I walked on until I came to the hedge that separated Millie's property from that of the Jacobs estate. Looking up at the treehouse, I thought I saw movement, but I wasn't sure. I waved anyhow, then turned around and made my way back.

Taking the "high road" as the path forked, I knew I would end up at the lookout getting to it from the back side. Climbing the last few yards of the steep hill, I spotted Michael ahead.

Chapter 28

Michael sat on a little folding stool, his eyes raised up to the lookout. An easel was propped up in front of him. He was obviously working on a painting. Concentrating on his artwork, he did not seem to hear my approach. Taking a few more steps in his direction gave me the opportunity to study his profile unobserved. His long brown hair was pulled back into his customary ponytail. He sported a long forehead, a pair of brown eyes, a straight and narrow nose and fairly full lips. Then I glanced at the painting in progress, and I was spellbound. He had depicted Millie, standing at the railing with that faraway look in her eyes, so typical of her. A little cry escaped me, and Michael turned around.

He said, "Have you been standing here long?"

I replied, "I first watched you work, and then I looked at the painting and couldn't help the exclamation. You've captured Millie's expression to perfection! The way she stands at the edge of the overhang, looking down at the ocean, is very realistic."

He said, "Yes. I think I've captured her well. The painting is not finished, of course. I'm filling in the details and background, but I have to stop soon. The lighting is not right anymore. There is too much sun overhead now. I'll try to finish it tomorrow morning."

I asked, "Did Millie pose for this?"

"Oh no. I did a rough sketch one day, when I saw Mildred up on the lookout. She did not notice me at the time. I want to surprise her with this painting. Her birthday is coming up."

Then he smirked at me and said, "I hear you're not the harmless lady you seemed!"

The way he said this, his charm was undeniable. I suddenly understood Millie's fascination with this man.

I said, "Oh?"

"I was told you are here on sleuthing business."

"Word sure gets around fast," I commented.

Then he looked at me seriously, saying, "You probably think me an opportunist, but I happen to love Mildred."

I replied, "Yes, I think you do." Then I inquired, "What is your opinion about Millie's fall?"

"I don't know. I guess it's possible that she was pushed. Like my mother would say, 'No smoke without fire.'"

"Does your mother live far away?"

Michael said, "No. She lives on the mainland, not very far from Long Beach."

"I was surprised she didn't come to your art exhibit."

Seemingly embarrassed, he replied, "Unfortunately, she could not make it to the event."

Then I said, "I enjoyed the show very much and was impressed with your talent."

"Thank you," he said modestly. And once again, I felt that he was essentially a shy man.

He added, "The exhibit has already stirred some interest in my work, I'm happy to say. I've sold two of my paintings so far as a result of the show, and Pamela informed me today that several prospective buyers have contacted her as well."

I said, "That's wonderful, Michael!" And I added, "So Pamela Norris is still in the picture. I assumed her job was done once the exhibit was over."

"Well, she kind of made herself my agent," he said.

"I see."

"Actually, I'm glad she takes care of the business part. I'm really not much good at that. Pamela tells me I tend to price the paintings much too low."

He looked up at the sky and stated, "It's just too bright. I'm quitting for today," and he started to gather all his stuff.

I suggested, "Let me help you carry some of the things back. You better take the painting yourself, though."

He grinned and said, "I wouldn't trust you with it anyhow!"

Chapter 29

◇◇◇◇◇◇◇◇◇◇◇◇◇◇◇◇◇◇◇◇◇◇

Back in my room in the late afternoon, I picked up my cell phone.

"Law Offices of Samuelson, Rosenbaum & Blight, how can I direct your call?"

"R.A. Huber speaking. Mr. Samuelson, please."

"What is this concerning?"

"I am a friend of Lillian Robertson, and I need to talk to Mr. Samuelson."

"One moment. I'll see if he can talk to you."

While on hold, I kept my fingers crossed. I had to cross them for a long time.

Finally, I heard a deep voice, "This is Steve Samuelson. You are Mrs. Huber, I presume. What is this all about?"

I said, "Thank you, Mr. Samuelson, for talking to me. I won't take up much of your time. I assume Lillian Robertson already called you today?"

"Yes, she did. Frankly, I would not have taken your call if Mrs. Robertson hadn't asked me to answer your questions. She is a long-standing client of this firm, and I'm honoring her wishes as such. Lillian Robertson did not tell me what the questions were about, so please get on with it, Mrs. Huber."

I said, "I understand Lillian's sister, Mildred Faracelli -- who is also my friend, by the way -- came to see you today."

He replied, "That is correct."

"Did Mildred Faracelli come to see you about a new will? I know you cannot tell me what is in the will. All I am asking is if she actually made a new will today."

There was a long pause, and then he said, "I have decided to answer your question. The wills were already drawn up according to Mrs. Faracelli's instructions. She just came to sign the documents today."

I said, "Did you say 'wills,' Mr. Samuelson?"

He replied, "Did I? That was a slip of the tongue. I meant will and trust. There is a living trust in conjunction with the will."

"I see."

"Anything else, Mrs. Huber?"

"No, that is all. Thank you very much, Mr. Samuelson."

After hanging up, I reflected on the conversation. Wills? A slip of the tongue from a lawyer? Interesting.

Lillian called me after dinner that evening.

I said, "Hi Lillie. Thanks for buttering up Mr. Samuelson for me! I got the information I wanted from him."

"I knew you would. I'm just calling to give you the Albertis address, before I forget. Then I'm going to bed. I've had a long day and I'm bushed."

I said, "I keep forgetting that you are three hours ahead of us."

After I had jotted down the address, she commented, "I can't imagine what you want from Mrs. Albertis."

I replied, "Oh, I might not even contact her, but there seems to be a bit of a mystery about the relationship between Michael and his mother. You know me: I don't like unsolved mysteries."

"That's a fact! So I'll count on you to solve the mystery surrounding Millie."

We said goodnight and hung up.

I lay awake that night, thinking about all the information I had gathered since staying in the Faracelli household. I tried to sort it out and make sense of it. The forlorn feeling I had experienced when Millie boarded the ship kept creeping back into my mind. My last thought before slumber overtook me was, "Level with me, Millie!"

Chapter 30

◇◇◇◇◇◇◇◇◇◇◇◇◇◇◇◇◇◇◇

Coming down for breakfast relatively early on Wednesday morning, I noticed most of the household members had already gathered around the dining room table.

I said, "Good morning! Another perfectly beautiful day!"

Millie said, "Good morning, Reg. Looks like everyone is up except Gina and Lisa."

Tony stated, "Lisa didn't feel well this morning, so she went back to bed."

Guido grinned and said, "I presume Gina had a late consultation with her doctor last night and needs her beauty sleep now."

Beatrix appeared with a pitcher of orange juice and a breadbasket.

She turned to Jesse and said, "I know you don't have a diving instruction today. Do you still want your Gatorade?"

He replied, "I might as well. I'm very thirsty."

Michael said, "I don't understand how anyone can drink Gatorade. That stuff tastes awful!"

Then Millie said to Jesse, "Sorry your diving lesson got cancelled. You don't get tutored on Wednesdays either. What are you planning to do today, Jesse?"

"I'll just hang with Julia, I guess."

Then Millie asked him, "Is there going to be a ceremony when you get your certification next Monday?"

"No. I guess the instructor will just hand it to me after the dive."

She announced, "Well, Jesse, I'm going to be there when you come up from that dive, and we'll have a little party and celebrate. You can invite anyone you wish."

His eyes lit up, and he said, "Thanks, Mom!"

Guido turned to Jesse, saying, "Once you are certified, I might consider becoming your buddy on some dives, if you behave yourself!" And he nudged him playfully.

"Cool," said Jesse.

Millie commented, "I didn't know you scuba dive, Guido."

Guido laughed, and said, "There is a lot you don't know about me, Mom!" He added, "Actually, I got certified a few years ago. I was heavily into diving for a while, but then, due to my all- consuming business pressures, could not find the time for it any longer."

Then Millie inquired, "What's everyone else up to today?"

Tony volunteered, "I think I'm going to spend some time on the computer. I need to do lots more research on the web regarding my prospective flight company."

Guido said, "I'm going to hit the road. I'll reserve a seat on the Catalina Express for this morning. I might as well tend to my business, while it still exists."

There was an awkward pause, and then Millie said, "I'm going to work on my bird. I want to finish it today and make it ready for shipping to the casters."

"In that case, I'm going to set up shop on the lookout," Michael said, and he winked at me.

Millie asked, "What are your plans, Reg?"

I answered, "I think I'll hike further up the road and see where it will take me."

Millie informed, "The road ends eventually. Did you bring hiking boots? I believe it gets pretty rugged further up the hill. You might run into some wild animal, as well."

I wasn't sure if she was serious or if she was making fun of me, so I ignored the wild animal remark and replied, "I'll manage in my tennis shoes."

Breakfast over with, I said good-bye to Guido, and we all went our separate ways.

Before going off on my little hike, I wrote a few postcards I had purchased in town. I addressed one of them to my daughter, reassuring her that all was well between her father and me. It was approximately nine o'clock when I headed up the road.

I walked past the Jacobs house, which looked to be more of a Mediterranean architecture than Spanish, with less exterior ornamentation and simpler lines. Further up, I came across one more estate on the north side of the road. After that, there were no more houses in sight. Just like Millie had predicted, I eventually came to the end of the road. I noticed a narrow hiking trail to the left and decided to explore further. I had packed my cell phone, just in case of wild animals, as well as bringing a small bottle of water along, so I felt pretty safe hiking on my own. Although I found myself among nature's tranquility and peace, my thoughts were anything but peaceful. I kept thinking of all the conversations I had had with everyone in the Faracelli household.

About an hour into my hike, I abruptly stopped and said aloud, "OK, Millie, I'm going to have it out with you! You are going to level with me, right now!"

I turned around and quickly walked back down the hill.

Chapter 31

◇◇◇◇◇◇◇◇◇◇◇◇◇◇◇◇◇◇◇

I opened the studio door without bothering to knock. I took a few steps towards the workbench and came to a sudden halt. A sharp cry escaped me. Millie was slumped back in her chair facing the bench. Her blouse was stained dark red on her left side. Looking at her immobile face, I was overcome by her expression of contentment and peace. In front of her sat the nearly finished exquisite bird. Sculpting materials and rags, as well as sgraffitos and other tools, were scattered on the bench, pieces of clay sticking to some of them. Knowing instinctively it was useless, I rushed to her anyhow, grabbed her wrist and felt for a pulse. There wasn't any.

I looked at my watch. It was 10:35. I glanced over at Millie's lifeless body once more and said a silent prayer. Then I stepped outside and yelled for the housekeeper.

Beatrix came out of the house and walked towards me, saying, "Did you call me?"

By that point I had myself in control, and I said, "I found Mrs. Faracelli murdered in her studio."

"Oh my God!"

I said, "Where is the key to the studio?"

She replied, "It's in the house."

"Bring it to me. Then call the police."

I waited by the studio door until Beatrix handed me the key. I locked the door to the studio, pocketed the key, and then followed her sadly into the house.

After Beatrix had called the authorities, she said, "Avalon's Deputy Sheriff, the lieutenant, will be here shortly."

Then she asked, "Are you sure Mrs. Faracelli is dead?"

I said, "Yes. I'm sure."

We were silent for a while, both of us still in shock.

Then she said, "How are we going to break this to the family?"

I replied, "There is no easy way to break the bad news. We just have to use our good judgment. I'm going to call Lillian Robertson in Boston first. Then I'll help you with informing the rest of the family."

Once in my room, I took a deep breath and then dialed Lillie's number.

After explaining the situation, I said, "Oh, Lillie. I've failed to prevent Millie's murder. I've let you both down. I am so sorry."

She replied, "Don't blame yourself, Reg. It's not your fault."

Then she stated, "I'll take the next flight to LAX. Let's see. It's a quarter till two, so that makes it a quarter till eleven your time. Hopefully I'll get there by this evening. Once in LA, I'll decide if I can catch the last boat to Catalina. If not, I'll arrive by helicopter. I'll let you know."

Coming down the stairs, Gina intercepted me, crying out, "Tell me it isn't true, Mrs. Huber!"

I said, "I'm afraid it is."

She ran past me up the stairs, sobbing. Then I heard her door slam.

Tony came toward me, white as a sheet, and said, "Beatrix just told me. I want to see Mom. Give me the key, Mrs. Huber."

I said, "I'm very sorry, Tony, but the door to the studio stays locked until the police get here."

He nodded and then headed for the stairs, saying, "I'll go up and tell Lisa."

At that moment the doorbell chimed. Beatrix went to answer it and ushered the lieutenant and his subordinate in. The senior deputy was a congenial looking middle-aged man; his underling was a tall young man in his twenties.

Introductions over with, the lieutenant asked, "Where is the victim?"

I gave him the key to the studio, and Beatrix showed them the way. The lieutenant came back to the house a short time later, leaving his officer stationed at the studio door. The deputy sheriff then wanted to know who had found the victim. He took me into the dining room and questioned me at length, going a little into my background, my relationship to Millie, and the events leading up to her tragic death. He then had me describe how I found her, what time it was when I found her, what the studio looked like upon my entry, et cetera. After he was done with me, he asked Beatrix to come into the room.

He said to both of us, "Are all the household members still on the premises?"

Beatrix answered, "Everyone except Guido Faracelli. He is on his way to the mainland. His sister, Gina, just came back a little while ago from dropping him off at the boat landing."

The lieutenant said, "Please assemble all the members of the household in this room. I want to talk to everyone. In the meantime, I'll call the authorities in Long Beach and have them send Mr. Guido Faracelli back to Avalon."

Beatrix said, "Tony, Lisa and Gina are in the house. I'll get them. I think Jesse is over at Julia's. I assume Michael is out painting somewhere."

I said to her, "Please call Julia's house and just say that there is an emergency and Jesse needs to come home. I'll wait at the hedge and break the news to him. I also know where to find Michael, so I'll inform him as well. Give me a few minutes before you call."

I found Michael as expected near the lookout, finishing his painting. After I had told him the sad news, he just stared at me incomprehensibly. When I told him the deputy sheriff wanted everyone to assemble in the dining room, the news started to sink in.

As I walked in the direction of the Jacobs property, Jesse was already on my side of the hedge and strode rapidly towards me, asking, "What's the emergency?"

As gently as I possibly could, I told him.

He said, "I don't believe you."

"It's true, Jesse."

He looked at me wide-eyed, and then his whole body started to shake. I put my arm around his shoulder and led him home.

As we entered the dining room, the rest of the family was already gathered except for Guido. My fanny pack was searched, and we were both frisked.

The lieutenant addressed us all, "You've all heard the shocking news of Mrs. Faracelli's murder. I am disturbed and shocked myself. I have asked our homicide squad team from the mainland to assist with this case. They are on their way and should be here shortly."

I got the feeling that the deputy sheriff was not used to murder on his peaceful island.

He continued, "All of you need to be ready for questioning, so please do not leave the premises. Do not go near the studio structure until after the team is done with it. My assistant is stationed there now. As a matter of fact, I am asking you all to stay inside the house until further notice."

So, for the time being, we were all under house arrest.

Chapter 32

We were still assembled in the dining room when the LA County Sheriff's homicide squad team arrived. Their top man looked to be in his thirties. He was of average height, with brown hair and eyes, and had a brusque, superior manner. He first talked to the lieutenant and then gave his subordinates specific instructions. The team of white-clad persons dispersed, presumably in the direction of the studio. Two uniformed men disappeared as well. Two other uniforms, the lieutenant and the "leader of the pack," remained in the room.

He then addressed us. "My name is Detective Ron Barker. I'm with the Los Angeles County Sheriff Homicide Squad. Our lieutenant here in Avalon asked for assistance with this case. I can imagine that this is a trying time for all of you, but I must insist on your cooperation by following my instructions. Our team is working on the crime scene right now. I am also sending a couple of my people to search all the rooms in the house. As a matter of routine, the officers here will take everyone's fingerprints. Please form a line. It will only take a few minutes. Thank you for your cooperation."

The two uniformed officers had already set up at the end of the table. One took each person's prints; the other handed out moist wipes after the job was done. Taking my turn, the thought occurred to me that my fingerprints were already on file. They had been taken at the occasion of my becoming a citizen of the United States, over thirty years ago. I kept quiet, however. Better not make any waves, I had decided. A little black ink wouldn't do me any harm.

Detective Barker continued, "I will question each one of you separately, and I'm asking everyone else to stay in this room until called."

He turned to Beatrix and asked, "Are you the housekeeper?"

"Yes."

"What is your name?"

"Beatrix Primrose."

"OK, Ms Primrose, in which room can I conduct the interviews? It doesn't need to be big, I just need a desk or table and three chairs."

Beatrix said, "The office would probably be best."

The detective said to her, "Please direct the officer to it," and he nodded at one of his minions.

He then looked around the dining room, walked over to the door connecting it with the living room, opened it, glanced into it, and then closed the door again. He then walked to the sliding glass door leading to the veranda, which stood open as usual during the day. He stepped outside, strolled around out there, and then came back in.

He commented, to no one in particular, "I see there is access to the patio from the living room too."

Beatrix and the uniform came back, and she said, "The office is ready."

The detective thanked her and nodded to his subordinates, who went in opposite directions.

Then he said to us, "Feel free to roam around in this room and on the patio, but no further, please. There is an officer stationed outside the door in the hallway, and another out by the patio. It is not that I don't trust you, but these are standard procedures."

Then he informed us, "The lieutenant and I will begin the questioning now. We'll start with you, Ms Primrose."

And turning to the rest of us, he added, "I will ask Ms Primrose to list everyone in the household for us, so we can call you all by name."

After the door shut behind Beatrix and the two law enforcers, there was no comment from anyone. We just sat in silence, each with our own thoughts of grief and worries. I studied each person of our little group. Tony seemed to have a hard time controlling his emotions. Lisa was stroking his hand in an effort to comfort him. Gina was quietly crying. Michael seemed oblivious to everyone around him. I turned to Jesse sitting next to me, and the desperate anguish and sorrow in his eyes was hard for me to take.

Tony was called for questioning next. Then it was Gina's turn.

After Tony took his seat in the dining room again, he burst out, "They won't let me see Mom. How can I believe that she's dead if I can't even see for myself?"

He looked straight at me and said, "Do you understand?"

I replied, "Yes. Tony. I understand. I would feel the same in your place."

At some point in the early afternoon, Beatrix asked one of the officers for permission to go to the kitchen and fix some lunch. She served us chicken salad and drinks, but nobody had an appetite.

When I went out to the veranda, unzipping my fanny pack, the officer stationed nearby glanced at me suspiciously. When he saw me take cigarettes and lighter out of it, he relaxed and shook his finger at me in a "naughty, naughty" gesture. I heard new movement coming from the dining room and then Guido's voice, "What the hell is going on?"

Then Tony's voice, "You mean they didn't tell you?"

"As soon as I arrived in Long Beach, a Catalina Express official intercepted me and told me I had to go back to Avalon because Mom was dead. Then, when I got here just now, a police officer told me I had to come to the dining room. I want to see Mom. What happened? Where is she?"

"She was murdered."

Guido yelled, "No! You're lying. Where is she?"

Tony said, "We're not allowed to leave this room until they tell us."

Going back inside, I saw Guido's astonished face. He looked at his older brother in utter disbelief and said, "You mean we are kept prisoners here?"

"Yes."

Guido had calmed down somewhat, then asked, "You said 'murdered'? Who the heck would want to murder Mom?" And he added, "Where?"

"In her studio."

"When?"

I said, "We don't know when, but I found her at 10:35."

Guido exclaimed, "Oh my God! I went to say good-bye to her a few minutes before ten o'clock. Someone must have killed her soon after that."

He sank into a chair and was silent.

At that moment Lisa came back from her interview and told Guido he was next.

Afterwards Michael was called, then Jesse, and it looked very much like they'd kept me for last.

When Jesse came back from his questioning, Detective Barker came into the room right after him, announcing, "We are done with the crime scene. I understand that some of you want to see the victim before she is taken away. You can do so in just a moment. The rooms have been searched, so you are all free to go. Be advised, though, that for the next few days, I want all of you to remain on the island." And looking at me, he added, "See you in the office in ten minutes, Mrs. Huber."

We all followed the detective out the back door. We encountered the team on the path between studio and house, pushing Millie on a gurney. As we came close, one of the white-clad people pulled back the sheet to expose Millie's head. She looked as peaceful as I had seen her earlier, and I said my last good-bye.

Chapter 33

Detective Barker and I started out on the wrong foot from the very beginning. The detective was already seated behind the desk when the lieutenant and I walked into the office. The lieutenant grabbed the chair next to him, while I was motioned into one across the desk.

Detective Barker said, "Now, then. You have already been questioned by the lieutenant here, so I'm going to make this as brief as possible. State your full name and age, please."

I complied, "My name is Regula Agatha Huber. I am 60 years old." And I added, "Professionally, I go by R.A. Huber."

He said, "Ah, yes. You claim to be a private eye."

I retorted, "I don't claim to be. I am a private detective. I have the papers to prove it."

"Whatever." Then he said, "I understand you told the lieutenant that you are here professionally. Correct?"

"Yes."

"Tell me how that came about."

I went into the whole story. I told him how I was approached and hired by Lillian Robertson; how her twin sister, Mildred Faracelli, invited me to stay with her on Catalina Island; and how I tried to figure out what was wrong in the household. I told him about Lillie's suspicion that her sister did not simply have a fall down the stairs last May, but that she might have been pushed.

My narrative concluded, the detective asked, "Did Mildred Faracelli report her attempted murder to the police at the time?"

I replied. "Mildred Faracelli was positive that she had simply lost her footing and had fallen down the stairs on her own."

With obvious sarcasm in his voice, he said, "Am I getting this right, R.A. Huber? Did you come here on an investigation because some woman told you she had 'bad vibes' about this household and that Mildred Faracelli might have been pushed down some stairs, even though Mrs. Faracelli herself said that she just fell?"

Annoyed, I said, "Yes. But not just some woman. It was the victim's twin sister. Obviously she was right, otherwise we would not have a victim."

"Where is Lillian Robertson, by the way? I definitely want to talk to her."

"She lives in Boston. I called her, and she is on her way. Hopefully she'll arrive at LAX in the early evening."

He asked, "When did you call her?"

I said, "Right after the housekeeper called you people."

"That was quick thinking, R.A. Huber!" he said, his voice dripping with sarcasm. Then he continued, "You are the one that discovered the body?"

"Yes, I did."

"Tell me your movements from the time you got up this morning until you discovered the body."

I told him in detail how I had found most of the household gathered around the breakfast table, the only ones absent having been Gina and Lisa. Then I started to tell him all about my little hike up the hill.

He interrupted and asked, "Why did you go on this hike of yours?"

I said, "No particular reason, other than to explore the neighborhood and get some exercise. I am used to working out, and I get restless when not physically active. Besides, walking stimulates my brain and I can think out problems best when doing so."

He said, "Please continue."

When I got to the point in my story of having stopped and turned back to talk to Millie, he said, "Why?"

I replied, "I had come to the conclusion that she knew something about this mystery but wasn't telling."

"Like what?"

"Obviously, Detective Barker, I was too late to find out."

When I explained how I had opened the door to the studio and found Millie dead, he inquired, "Did you touch the victim?"

I said, "Yes. I touched her wrist and felt for a pulse, even though I knew beforehand I would not find any sign of life."

"Why did you check anyhow?" he asked.

"I can't explain it, I just had to do it."

He nodded, and said, "Yes. That, I can understand. It is a normal reaction under the circumstances."

This comment took me by surprise, and I realized that Detective Ron Barker could be quite human after all.

Then he questioned me further, "Did you touch anything in the studio?"

"No."

"I heard that you locked the studio door after you had discovered the victim. Where was the key kept?"

"It was kept in the house. I asked Beatrix to fetch it."

He said, "Where were you when she went to get the key?"

I replied, "I stood by the studio door, to make sure no one would enter it."

"Very clever of you," he commented.

At that point, I could not tell if he meant it or if he was mocking me.

Then he said, "So you are sure that from the time you locked that door to the time you handed the key to the deputy sheriff, nobody went into the studio?"

"Yes. I am sure."

He continued, "In your opinion, how was Mildred Faracelli murdered?"

I said, "As far as I could see, she was stabbed in the heart."

"How do you know?"

"She had been bleeding profusely from a wound in her heart area. Her blouse was stained dark red. There was no bullet hole visible, so I deduced that she had been stabbed."

He said, "Can you make a guess of approximately how long she had been dead when you found her?"

I replied, "Not long, I think. Rigor mortis had not set in. Her wrist was not ice cold to the touch yet. I am not an expert on the subject, so I would rather not take a guess as to how long."

"In your statement to the lieutenant you informed him that when you discovered the victim, the time was 10:35. Did you just happen to look at your watch before you went inside the studio?"

"No. I purposely looked at my watch when I was inside and had just found Millie."

"I see." Then he asked, "During your brain-stimulating hike, did you come to any conclusions?"

He was clearly having a heyday with me, and I was determined not to show my aggravation.

I answered politely, "Nothing definite."

There was a long pause while the man studied me. Then he asked, "Do you have a permit to carry your pistol?"

I said, "Certainly," and I reached into my fanny pack, found the wallet and handed him the permit.

He glanced at it and then gave it back, saying, "Seems in order." Then he asked, "Do you usually carry the pistol on your person?"

I replied, "No, actually very seldom. I only carry it when I feel there is a possibility that I or someone else is in danger."

"Why did you bring it on the island?"

"I brought it just in case I might need it. After all, I came here on a job."

He gave me a funny look and commented, "You might have a heck of a time getting at it in a hurry, stored in the back of a closet inside a bag which is kept inside a suitcase! What good your ammunition can do amongst your underwear, I can't imagine!"

By that time I was really mad and exclaimed, "Give me a break, Detective! When I first came to this house, no one knew that I was a private eye. I had expected my room to be vacuumed and dusted, and I did not want to advertise my gun. Had I known that the place was going to be searched by the police, I would have either carried my gun or found a hiding place which not even your minions could discover."

I think he was more amused than angry when he replied, "No need to get feisty, Mrs. Huber!"

At that moment I happened to glance at Avalon's deputy sheriff, who was actually grinning.

Detective Barker said, "OK. That is all for the time being, Mrs. Huber. Thank you." And he added, "I want to remind you not to leave the island until further notice."

I said, "I have no plans to leave until my job is finished."

He raised an eyebrow and stated, "We are in charge now."

I retorted, "I was hired by Lillian Robertson to find out if someone wanted to harm her sister. Now that her sister was murdered, I aim to find out who killed her. Unless Lillian Robertson fires me, I consider myself still on the job."

I got up and walked out the door.

Chapter 34

◇◇◇◇◇◇◇◇◇◇◇◇◇◇◇◇◇◇◇

Lillie had caught the 5:30 PM boat out of Long Beach. I picked her up one hour later in Avalon.

As she disembarked, I stepped forward, and we silently embraced. We both had a hard time holding back the tears.

I grabbed her suitcase and said, "I am so very sorry, Lillie. I wish I could have prevented it." And I added, "I haven't cashed your check. I'll return it to you."

She replied, "Don't be silly, Reg. Like I told you on the phone, it's not your fault."

As we made our way to where the golf cart was parked, she said, "Tell me what happened."

I gave her a brief account of that day's sad occurrence.

She asked, "How are the kids doing?"

I said, "They all seem very upset. I think Jesse is taking it the hardest. He was just coming to terms with himself, totally shaping up as far as the drugs are concerned, and starting to get a grip on life. Losing the only mother he knows is a hard blow to him."

As we were driving up the hill, she said, "So the police have already questioned everyone?"

I replied, "Everyone present at the house, yes."

"Are they collaborating with you?"

"Far from it. Detective Barker of the homicide squad does not believe my story," I said.

"What do you mean?"

"When he questioned me, I was under the impression that he considers me a suspect. I have the feeling he thinks I made up this tale about looking into 'something wrong' with the household."

Lillie said, "That's ridiculous!"

I said, "From his point of view, I can understand it. I am the only outsider, and making up this story would give me a reason for being here."

"Didn't you tell him that I hired you?"

"Yes, of course. But he might think I made you up as well."

Lillie said, "Well, I'll set him straight on that."

As we rounded the last curve before the house came into view, she said, "Please stay on the case for me, Reg."

"Oh, I'm planning to," I replied.

Chapter 35

A sad and dispirited group of people sat at the dinner table that night. Beatrix had served us a simple meal of cold cuts, assorted cheeses and bread, but nobody felt like eating.

Jesse, looking very pale, jumped out of his seat and said, "May I be excused?" And not waiting for an answer, he bolted out the door.

Lisa said, "Poor kid. He is having such a hard time, it's affected his stomach."

Guido remarked, "Either that or he has a bad conscience."

Gina said, "Don't be vulgar, Guido."

Guido stated, "Vulgar or not, I just want to know which one of us murdered Mom."

"Don't be ridiculous. We all loved her."

"That is exactly what I said to Mrs. Huber the other day, but someone must have had a love-hate relationship with her."

Lisa begged, "Let's not talk about this. It is up to the police."

Guido retorted, "The police might drag this out for weeks. I need to find out what happened to Mom now. When Barker interviewed me, I wanted to know how she was killed. He snubbed me and reminded me that he was the one who asked the questions."

He turned to me and asked, "You saw her without a sheet pulled over her. How did she die?"

I replied, "I am certain she was stabbed in the heart." And I added, "I think death came quickly and she did not have to suffer."

Michael, who had been totally silent until then, commented, "Thank God for that."

Guido continued, "Everyone sitting at this table had the opportunity to kill Mom today, with the exception of Aunt Lillian, who was in Boston. As far as motives" - -

Tony, glaring at his younger brother angrily, interrupted, "Cut it out, Guido, you're upsetting everyone."

Guido shot back, "We have to face facts. One of us is a murderer."

Lisa said, "A stranger could have walked down from the street and into the studio."

Guido said, "My dear Lisa, be realistic. The only logical suspects are the family, Michael, Mrs. Huber, Beatrix and Charles."

Gina protested, "What do you mean by Charles?"

"Well, sis, he could have come on the property undetected, and he has an indirect motive."

"You're crazy! What possible motive could Charles have?" she exclaimed.

Guido said, "I admit, it's a little far fetched, but he is your future husband and you'll inherit enough money to finance his lab. I can think up a motive for everyone." And turning to his brother, he said, "Let's start with you, Tony. An inheritance comes in real handy at the moment, furnishing you with the capital needed for starting your flying venture."

Tony shouted, "How dare you accuse me! What about you? As far as I know, Mom has turned your request for a loan down."

Lillie held up her hand and commanded, "Enough!"

She had shocked the two young men into silence with her authoritative order.

After a pause, she continued, "It is unproductive at the moment to make any kind of speculations. The only thing to do at this point is to give the police our full cooperation.

I have hired Reg to investigate as well. She is good at detecting and will find out the truth."

Before going to bed that night, I called Peter and informed him of the sad news.

"Oh, Regula. I am so sorry," he said.

Then he added, "I hope you don't blame yourself?"

I replied, "Of course I blame myself. I should have been able to prevent it."

"Do you have an idea of who murdered her?"

"Just an inkling, but nothing definite yet."

Peter said, "I assume the police have been on the scene?"

"Oh, yes," I replied, "First the Senior Deputy Sheriff of Avalon, a lieutenant, questioned us, and then the homicide team from the mainland, headed by Detective Ron Barker, showed up."

"So they actually called separate people in from the mainland?"

I stated, "No. They're not a separate outfit. Catalina Island is in Los Angeles County, and so Detective Ron Barker and his homicide squad are from the LA County Sheriff's Department also. They're all deputy sheriffs and work for the same agency."

There was a pause, and then Peter said, "If you want some moral support, I'll come to Catalina."

I replied, "I appreciate the offer, but at this point it might complicate matters."

"I don't get you."

"Well, we don't want to confuse the police and add another suspect to their list."

He said, "Yes. I see. Theoretically you are a suspect."

I retorted, "Not just theoretically. At the moment I seem to be suspect number one!"

"You've got to be kidding!"

"I'm serious. Detective Barker seems to think I made the whole story up. He does not believe I came here to find any 'bad vibes.'"

"I get it. As far as he's concerned, you are the convenient outsider."

"Exactly. On top of that, I was the one who discovered the body. That in itself is suspicious."

Then I added, "Lillie got here tonight. She'll confirm my story to the police."

Peter commented, "That will clear things up for you, Regula."

"Unless Detective Barker will conclude that Lillie and I are in cahoots!"

Peter asked, "What kind of a guy is this Barker, anyhow?"

I replied, "He is young and full of himself. However, I judge him to be good at his job." And I added, "I am under the impression that he does not like private eyes in general, and me in particular."

"Was he rude to you?"

"No. He was actually very polite in a condescending way, if you understand what I mean."

"Yes. I get the picture." Then he inquired, "How is the family reacting?"

I answered, "From what I can tell, they are all devastated and are suffering, each in his or her own way. I honestly feel that Millie was truly loved by everyone. Guido's reaction shows up in anger and frustration. Jesse seems hit the hardest, I think. I feel very strongly for that boy."

Peter advised, "Now Regula, don't get too personally involved."

"I can't help it. I am personally involved," I replied.

Chapter 36

At 7:30 the next day, I found Lillie at breakfast. Her food untouched, an open address book in front of her, she was busily copying down names and phone numbers.

Looking up at my approach, she said, "Good morning, Reg." And she added, "I have to get on the ball and contact people. I'm just waiting for a decent time in the morning to call."

I sympathized, "Yes, of course. You have to make arrangements."

Then I asked, "Do you know if Millie had any specific instructions in her will, as far as the funeral arrangements go?"

Lillie replied, "I don't know if she mentioned it in her will, but I do know what her wishes were. She told me on one of my visits to California. At the time I thought it strange that she would be thinking about her death, but now I am glad to know what arrangements to make."

I said, "Was this on your recent visit to Avalon?"

"No. It was at the beginning of the year, January or February, at her house in South Pasadena. When Millie brought it up, I laughed at her and said, 'We are the same age. What makes you think I'll be around when you pass away?' She just gave me her typical mysterious smile."

As Lillie said this, a tear was slowly running down her face. She brushed it away, saying, "I can't let myself mourn just yet; I have too much to take care of." Then she continued, "Her wishes were actually very simple. She wanted to be cremated and her ashes buried here. I remember her exact words: 'No matter where I die, I want my ashes to be put to rest up on the lookout at my house on Catalina.'"

I nodded and said, "I can understand that."

At that moment Beatrix walked into the room and, addressing Lillie, said, "Bruce Dillon is scheduled to tutor Jesse this morning. Shall I call him and cancel?"

Lillie thought about it for a second, then answered, "Have him come. It might be best for Jesse to keep to his normal routine. Please call Mr. Dillon, though, and inform him of what has happened."

After Beatrix left, I said, "I agree with you, Lillie. Even if there won't be much accomplished as far as academics go, the tutor might be able to help Jesse emotionally. I've met Mr. Dillon and found him to be a very dedicated and understanding teacher."

Then I said, "Coming back to the task of your arrangements, is there going to be a ceremony of any kind?"

Lillie replied, "This weekend, probably on Saturday, we'll have a memorial service at a local church. I will organize it with the pastor, of course, before I call everyone. It will have to be Saturday or Sunday. You can't expect people to come to the island during the week. Whenever the authorities release Millie's body, the cremation will take place. Then, we, just the family and very close friends, will bury her ashes up at the lookout."

I commented, "You have given this a lot of thought already."

She said, "I couldn't sleep last night, so I had plenty of time to think."

We both sat in silence, making an attempt to get some food down. Then Lillie looked at her watch.

She said, "Almost 8 o'clock. I'll start making some of my calls, before the police get here. Beatrix told me they'd come at 9:00 AM."

As Lillie made the first call, presumably to the minister, I left the room to give her some privacy.

I had not gotten much sleep myself the night before, so I went up to my room to rest. I tried to read but could not concentrate. My thoughts centered on Millie and her tragic death. I mulled over all the exchanges of conversations with Millie, as well as with the rest of the people concerned, over the last week. The picture of finding her stabbed in the studio kept flashing in my mind.

I finally dosed off, and not used to taking naps, I woke up with a headache.

It was already afternoon when I came downstairs again. Gina was with Lillie, helping her with the arrangements, I presumed.

Lillie glanced at me, saying, "You look disoriented, Reg."

I replied, "I can't believe it. I actually fell asleep." I added, "I should have made myself useful and helped you instead."

She said, "We're just about done with the calling. We reached most people and left messages for the others."

Then I asked, "Are the police here?"

Lillie said, "Yes. When they first got here, they went into the studio. Then they interviewed me. After that, they headed over to that neighbor girl's house. Right now, they're questioning Mr. Dillon in the office."

I said, "They went to interrogate Julia?"

Gina said, "I guess to check out Jesse's alibi."

"I see."

The door opened, and Detective Barker stuck his head in, saying, "We are breaking for lunch. Then we'll stop at Dr. Timble's practice. We'll be back in the late afternoon."

Chapter 37

I was called to the office once more in the early evening. The lieutenant and Detective Barker were both seated behind the desk when I entered and took my place in the 'hot seat.'

The detective stated, "We need to cover some more ground with you, Mrs. Huber."

Aware of a slight change in Detective Barker's manner toward me, I said, "I take it you have questioned Lillian Robertson?"

He replied, "Yes, we have."

"And you came to the conclusion that she and I are not totally cuckoo?"

He managed a hint of a smile and said, "I found Lillian Robertson to be very sane and capable. She confirmed your story 100%."

He continued, "We checked you out, R.A. Huber. You are on record."

Surprised, I said, "You must be extremely thorough, finding a speeding ticket from three years ago!"

"I am not talking about any traffic offense. Your name popped up in the Worthington case."

"Oh, I see."

Then he said, "I happen to know Sergeant Wolf from the South Pasadena Homicide Squad personally. So I called him. He thinks very highly of you. He also described you to a 'T', so we are sure you are the person you claim to be!"

I said, "Does that mean I am no longer your main suspect?"

"What makes you think you ever were?"

"Come now, Detective. I was the convenient outsider, and you did not believe my story."

With a perfect poker face he said, "We had to take everyone into consideration as a suspect."

Then he said, "Mrs. Robertson informed us that she hired you, and she insists that you stay on the case. As a rule, I don't like to compare notes with private detectives, but since it is a fact that you are going to stay in this household regardless, I might as well make use of you. So keep your eyes open, R.A. Huber."

I said, "Yes, sir."

"Now to the questions. Did you see or hear anyone when coming back from your hike?"

"I did not see anyone. I heard the faint noise of a vacuum cleaner sounding from somewhere within the house."

He continued, "When the lieutenant told you and the housekeeper to bring everyone into the dining room, you stated that you knew where to find Michael Albertis. Did you see him on the lookout when you came back from your hike?"

"No. I was coming from the street and walked along the house and then in the direction of the studio. I could not have seen him. He had stationed himself on the back side of the lookout."

Detective Barker prompted, "So how did you know where he was?"

I replied, "I had seen him painting on that spot on Tuesday. Then yesterday, we were all sitting at the breakfast table, discussing what everyone's plans were for the day. Michael mentioned that he was going to finish the painting up by the lookout."

He questioned further, "Is there anything you can tell us concerning the crime scene or the victim, not previously mentioned?"

I said, "There was no sign of any struggle, and I was puzzled by the victim's expression of total peace and contentment."

"You noticed that, huh?"

I continued, "I know that suicide is out of the question. The weapon had been pulled out of the wound. I checked, without touching anything, if it had possibly fallen out of her hand. I could not see anything with the slightest bit of blood anywhere near her, or in the rest of the room, for that matter."

"There is no doubt, it was murder." And he added, "Why did you think of suicide? Was Mildred Faracelli depressed and unhappy?"

"Oh no. My friend was always happy. No matter what hardships fate brought her way, she always managed to make the best of a situation. I was just surprised by the peaceful expression on her face. I have not seen many murder victims, but I assume there would be a certain amount of horror, fear, pain, or at least surprise showing."

The detective said, "Yes. You are right. This victim's expression was unusual. The only way I can explain it is that she was totally unaware of the murderer's intent up to the last second. Death came very fast, by the way, so the emotional reaction might not have traveled to her brain fast enough."

I said, "May I ask you a few things?"

He said, "You can ask, but I might not tell you."

"Have you received the medical examiner's report yet?"

"Yes, we have."

"Can you give me a short summary?"

He thought about this for a few seconds, and then he said, "I don't see what harm it can do. Here are the main facts: The victim was stabbed in the aorta, the main artery gate to the heart. The weapon was pushed between ribs and pierced the aorta. Blood spurted out instantly, decreasing the amount going to the brain and to the rest of the body. Death occurred within two to three minutes. According to body temperature, the victim expired one to two and a half hours before medical examination took place on the scene at 11:18 AM."

I did a quick calculation, and then said, "So she was killed roughly between 8:50 and 10:20."

"Correct."

Then I inquired, "Have you found the murder weapon?"

He replied, "We're working on it."

"Would a tool with a sharp point of about two to three inches suffice to pierce the aorta?"

Detective Barker raised an eyebrow and said, "What do you have in mind?"

"A variety of sculpting tools were laying on the workbench. I noticed the only one without any clay sticking to it was a sgraffito tool, which had a two-or three-inch needle-point."

Avalon's deputy sheriff, who had been silent until then, said, "You are very observant, Mrs. Huber."

Then he turned to the detective, asking, "Have the sculpting tools been considered as possible murder weapons?"

The detective answered, "Yes. They have been taken to the lab. The result is pending."

Then he looked back at me and said, "You think the sgraffito without any trace of clay is the murder weapon. Why did you single that one out amongst all the other tools?"

I replied, "There was no blood on any of the tools, at least not visible. So I figured the murderer might have washed the weapon in the sink, then wiped it clean and dry with one of the rags, and replaced it on the workbench. As I said, the only clean-looking tool was that sgraffito."

He said to me accusingly, "Why didn't you tell us about this theory of yours when we questioned you yesterday?"

I shrugged and replied, "At that time, I was under the impression I might be suspect number one. I felt it wiser to keep any theories about murder weapons to myself."

The lieutenant chuckled and said, "She's got you there!"

Detective Barker, far from being amused, continued, "Since we are picking your brain about theories, why would the murderer bother to wash the weapon and put it back on the workbench?"

"I've thought about that," I said. "The murderer wanted to put it back, because it might be missed otherwise. I presume he or she wore rubber gloves. So after the stabbing, it was easier to wash the gloves and murder weapon all at once without getting blood on his or her person."

He said, "Yes. I see. The lab team informed me that the murderer had been extremely neat. They found a slight trace of blood in the sink, nothing that could be seen with the naked eye, though. Lots of blood was on the victim, but none was found in the room."

He continued, "If your idea is correct, I can't imagine where the murderer discarded the gloves and the rag. We searched every person, as well as the grounds and all the rooms in the house."

I said, "I noticed the trash pick-up people drive up the hill just as I got back to the house after my hike."

The detective stated, "Oh, great. So these items might have been put into the trash bin outside and are, of course, long gone by now."

After a pause, he said, "I expect the lab report on the sculpture tools at any moment. We'll soon find out if your hunch was correct." Then he said, "Can you enlighten us about anything else?"

"I can't think of anything more," I replied.

Some of his mocking manner of the previous day showed again as he said, "You don't have a theory of who the murderer might be?"

"Not yet." And I inquired, "Can anyone be ruled out? I mean does anyone have a proven alibi?"

He said, "Nope." Then he opened his folder, looked at his notes, and read: "Beatrix Primrose claimed she was cleaning house the entire time. She could easily have gone to the studio and back at some point. Tony Faracelli stated he was in the office all morning doing flight research on the Internet. He could have sneaked out for a few minutes. His wife was apparently in bed sleeping. We have no proof of that. Gina Faracelli was sleeping late as well. No witnesses in her bed either. She had breakfast at 9:30 and drove her brother down to the boat docks at approximately 10:00. Guido Faracelli told us he had been in the den, making business calls, then packed his bags and went to say good-bye to his mother at approximately 9:50. He claims she was alive and well at that time. Nobody saw him the entire morning, until he asked his sister to drive him down to Avalon.

"Jesse Limburg spent the morning at his friend's house, Julia Jacobs. The girl confirms this. If she is to be believed, Jesse is the only one with an alibi. Michael Albertis was up by the lookout, painting. Jesse actually saw him there, looking over from the treehouse located at the Jacobs residence. Of course, the boy did not keep a steady watch on him. "R.A. Huber was" - - he looked at me. "No need to go into all that. I interviewed the tutor, Bruce Dillon, who stated he was home, making love to his wife. No witnesses to that event either. Gina's fiancé, Dr. Charles Timble, claimed he saw his first patient of the day at 9:45. Before that, he apparently was at his home alone.

"So, as you can see, nobody concerned has a verified alibi. With maybe the exception of Jesse, everyone is a suspect."

I winked at him and said, "Thank you for leaving me out of the picture!"

The lieutenant put in, "Amazing how nobody in the household seemed to have come across anyone else during the crucial time of approximately one and a half hours."

I stated, "It is really not all that amazing; I myself did not see anyone after I came back from my hike. Don't forget, everyone's plans for the morning were established at breakfast. So except for Lisa and Gina, who apparently were still in bed, everyone knew where each person was going to be. The two women could easily have questioned Beatrix later as to the whereabouts of the household."

Then Detective Barker said, "I understand you've been in the Faracelli household for one week?"

"Yes."

"Can you think of anyone else you've come in contact with concerning this family during that time?"

I replied, "There was an art exhibits coordinator, Pamela Norris, organizing things around here for an art show, which took place last Saturday at the Casino Ballroom. But that might be a little far-fetched."

"Might be, but she was apparently in this house the morning of the murder."

Surprised, I said, "She was?"

"The housekeeper told us that the art exhibit person was here to talk to Mildred Faracelli at about 8:30 and left shortly afterwards. Tony Faracelli confirmed this. According to him, he and his mother had lingered in the dining room after their breakfast, when Pamela Norris dropped by. She apparently left before the earliest possible time the crime could have been committed. Theoretically, she could have come back later, waited for an unobserved moment, walked down from the street, past the house and into the studio. She is on our list to be questioned. We just haven't gotten around to it yet."

Then he asked, "Anyone else?"

"No. I can't think of anyone else."

"That's it, then. Thank you."

I was let go.

Chapter 38

◇◇◇◇◇◇◇◇◇◇◇◇◇◇◇◇◇◇◇◇

Waking up Friday morning, I had a strong urge for physical activity. I missed my gym and felt a competitive game of racquetball would suit me best. Since that was not an option on the island, I settled for a jog.

Heading out my door, I gathered the postcards I had written Wednesday morning, planning to drop them into a mailbox in town. I presumed the police had read them and copied down the recipient's addresses. Since my life is an open book, I was not bothered by that fact.

My jogging routine completed, I had worked up an appetite and was eager for food. I stood at the center of town, contemplating which restaurant to choose, when Lisa walked up to me, saying, "Want to join me for breakfast, Mrs. Huber?"

I said, "Lisa! Are you by yourself?"

"Yes," she answered. "I could not take the gloomy atmosphere at the house anymore and just took off. I doubt anyone will miss me, unless Jesse wants to use his golf cart. I took the green one, which I think is his."

Seated at a table for two, I said, "You look upset, Lisa. Breakfast will do you good."

She complained, "I needed to get away. People in the Faracelli house are starting to get on my nerves. Guido stares at everyone suspiciously. Gina is getting touchy as well. Michael seems to be in a daze. I can't bear to look at poor Jesse. Even Beatrix has lost her cool and is dropping dishes. Lillian is a very nice lady, but she is busy with making arrangements and can't be bothered."

I stated, "All understandable, under the circumstances."

"Oh, I know. It's just hard to take after a while."

I studied her and then said, "You did not mention Tony. What happened between you and Tony?"

She admitted, "You guessed it. We had a fight. Actually, it wasn't really a fight. I just got my feelings hurt. I don't think Tony even realized it. I seem to be more sensitive during my pregnancy."

"That comes with the territory." And I added, "Tell me what happened."

"It's really rather silly, and I shouldn't have gotten so upset. We were in our room getting dressed to go downstairs, and I wanted to get Tony's input about what to name our baby. He said, 'How can you think about baby names at a time like this?' He hurt my feelings. So instead of following him down for breakfast, I went to the garage, got into a golf cart and drove myself down here."

I said, "I can sympathize with both of you."

The waitress served our breakfast: French toast for Lisa, bacon and eggs for me.

"You'll feel better as soon as you take some nourishment," I commented.

We ate our food in agreeable silence.

Then I said, "Let's discuss baby names."

Surprised, Lisa asked, "You really want to? I know you have other things on your mind right now."

"I can't think about solving the murder mystery every waking minute, or I'd drive myself crazy." Then I stated, "We are looking for boy names. Am I right?"

"Yes. How did you know? I don't think I mentioned it."

"I took a guess. And since there are only two possibilities, I had a 50% chance of guessing correctly."

"You are funny, Mrs. Huber."

We tried to think of names that would sound good with Faracelli. We went through the whole alphabet in turn. Some of the names I came up with sounded comical, bordering on bizarre. By the time we got to the letter Z, I had Lisa laughing hysterically.

On leaving the restaurant, she said, "I actually had fun and forgot about our troubles!"

I commented, "Laughing is good for you and for the baby!"

Chapter 39

◇◇◇◇◇◇◇◇◇◇◇◇◇◇◇◇◇◇◇

In the afternoon I was sitting out on the veranda, browsing through *The Catalina Islander* and *The Avalon Bay News*, the two local weekly news publications. Lillie came out and joined me, cup of coffee in hand.

I asked, "Did you get a chance to read *The Catalina Islander*?"

She said, "Millie's murder is mentioned on the front page, I know. It's also in *The Avalon Bay News* and the *Los Angeles Times*. I guess that sort of thing can't be avoided. The public has a right to know." And she added, "Millie being well known in art circles, there probably will be further write-ups. I just hope the reporters won't drag her life story through the mud."

Then she said, "Yesterday I distributed obituaries to the papers. They are probably listed in today's issues as well."

I inquired, "Are most of the arrangements settled?"

"Yes. Things are pretty much under control. The memorial service is scheduled for tomorrow at noon. This will give people a chance to catch the late-morning boat over here and get oriented in town. After the memorial service at the church, I have arranged for a luncheon at a restaurant in Avalon. As I told you before, the cremation will take place at a later date. Since we'll bury the ashes with just the family present, we'll play that by ear and no planning ahead is necessary."

Then she said, "I had a talk with Beatrix. I asked her to please stay with us until things are settled. She graciously agreed. That is a relief. I doubt this household could function without her." She continued, "I have not contacted the estate lawyers yet. There is no great hurry with that. I'll give them a call next week."

I said, "You mean everyone knows what to expect?"

She replied, "Yes. Millie has never made a secret about her will. Her fortune will be equally divided among all her stepchildren."

I said, "Speaking of which, have you given any thought of what to do about Jesse?"

Lillie looked at me, exasperated, and said, "I've been thinking of nothing else since Wednesday. I really don't know what's best for him. At first I thought I would just take him home to Boston with me, but the more I think about it, the more I realize that it would probably be the wrong decision. The boy might not be happy taken out of his environment."

I commented, "Yes. I believe you're right."

She continued, "He only has one more year of high school, and then he'll probably move to some college campus anyhow. He might be better off staying in California for this coming school year. I have a friend who lives in the general Pasadena area that would probably love to take him in. With his recent record, I doubt that the authorities would allow him to live by himself. I'll sit down with Jesse and discuss the options with him in a few days. Right now, he has enough of a burden to deal with Millie's death."

At that moment Beatrix came to announce that Detective Barker wanted Mrs. Robertson in the office. A little while later Tony and Lisa, holding hands, came from the direction of the rose garden and strolled toward me.

I said, "I'm happy to see you two have made up! Come, sit down and keep me company."

Tony glanced at the newspapers sitting on the table and said, "I was able to think of other things for a short time, but these" - - he pointed at the papers - - "are setting me back to deal with reality."

I said, "Tony, do you mind if I ask you a few questions about Wednesday morning?"

He replied, "I've told the police everything I know."

"Oh, I am sure you have, but they don't collaborate with me much."

"OK," he agreed.

"I understand you stayed and chatted with your mom when everyone else had dispersed after breakfast?"

"Yes. I talked to her again about my airline plans."

I inquired, "Did she agree to lend you money for your venture?"

He replied, "She did not give me an answer either way. She said she would have to think about it some more."

"I see." Then I asked, "I heard Pamela Norris came for a visit. How long did she stay?"

"Oh, just for about five minutes. It wasn't exactly a visit. Ms Norris just dropped by on her way down to Avalon."

I said, "Doesn't Ms Norris live on the mainland?"

He answered, "Yes, she does. If I remember correctly, she said that she had been on the island on personal business and just stopped by on her way to town to catch the boat back."

"Did she say where she had been coming from?"

"No."

I continued, "So Pamela Norris just came here to be social?"

"No, it wasn't a social call. She definitely wanted something from Mom," he said.

"Oh?"

"They actually had quite a heated argument. Apparently Ms Norris represented a client who was interested in buying one of Mom's sculptures."

"Which one?"

"That big head of Michael's."

I said, "Go on with the story, please."

He continued, "There isn't much to tell. Mom said the sculpture was not for sale. Pamela tried to make her change her mind, offering an enormous amount of money for the piece, on behalf of her client. Mom said no again and told the coordinator that she wished the sculpture had never been shown to the public."

I said, "You mentioned a heated argument. Who was actually angry?"

He answered, "I think they both were annoyed with each other, but Pamela was clearly mad. I remember her last words thrown at Mom, as she headed for the door: 'I'll be back! I always get my way in the end!'"

Lisa said, "Why would she get angry? What's it to her? She can just tell her client that the piece is not for sale."

Tony said, "I guess she had already counted on a big commission."

Lisa commented, "Everything always comes down to money."

"It seems that way," I said.

Chapter 40

◇◇◇◇◇◇◇◇◇◇◇◇◇◇◇◇◇◇◇◇

In the early evening that Friday, I was facing the two law enforcers again. The lieutenant sat relaxed in his chair, as usual, while Detective Barker did the talking.

He started by saying, "We have the lab report of the sculpting tools. You are correct in your theory, R.A. Huber. The sgraffito tool you described was the weapon used to stab Mildred Faracelli." Then he asked, "Has anything new occurred to you, since our talk of yesterday?"

I answered, "Not really. I talked to Tony this afternoon, and he told me about Pamela Norris dropping by on the morning of the murder."

The detective put in, "We questioned her this morning at her house before we started out to Long Beach for the boat trip over here."

I continued, "She had told Mildred and Tony she was stopping by on her way down to Avalon for her boat ride home. I couldn't help but wondering where the art exhibit coordinator could have been coming from at 8:30 AM. As I found out on my hike, nothing much goes on further up the road. There are exactly two more houses and then nothing but wilderness."

He laughed and said, "I can enlighten you about that mystery. When we questioned her, she reluctantly gave us the information. She came from the Jacobs residence. She is apparently Mr. Jacobs's girlfriend."

I exclaimed, "Pamela Norris is Julia's father's girlfriend! It's a small world after all!"

Then Detective Barker said, "She was probably on her way to catch the same boat as Guido Faraccelli. I asked her if they had seen each other on the Catalina Express, but she claimed they don't know one another."

I said, "That's possible. Guido did not arrive on the island until Sunday, so he missed the art exhibit. If he did not meet her on some previous occasion, they are strangers."

He continued, "We learned from Mrs. Robertson that all the Faracellis and the kid, Jesse, are Mildred Faracelli's heirs. Do you know if any of them are in desperate need of money?"

"Yes. All of them, except Jesse," I said.

Then I proceeded to tell him a short version of what I knew about the Faracelli children's financial problems. I also informed him of Dr. Timble's need for a loan.

He asked, "So they all approached their stepmother for a loan and were refused?"

"Not refused, just put off until later. My friend herself told me that eventually she would come to their aid but wanted to let them stew for a while."

"I see. But the result is the same. They did not get any money."

I commented, "I think they knew their mother well enough to know that she would help them in time."

"Maybe."

The deputy sheriff of Catalina opened his mouth for the first time that day, saying, "I knew Mildred Faracelli personally. She was a sweet lady, and I am positive she was planning to help her sons and daughter out."

I sent a grateful glance his way.

Detective Barker looked at his watch and stated, "That's it for today. My helicopter leaves in 25 minutes. I need to get out of here."

Chapter 41

When packing my all-occasion little black dress ten days before, I certainly didn't have a memorial service for Millie in mind. Guido and I were on our way down to the church in Avalon. I was driving the red-painted suntop golf cart.

Guido said, "Thanks for letting me come with you. I didn't want to share the ride with a potential murderer."

I replied, "So you think I'm excluded as a suspect?"

"Come now, Mrs. Huber. We both know this was an inside job. What upsets me most is the fact that the murderer is one of the family."

"How can you be sure?"

"It stands to reason that we have to look amongst one of the persons present when Mom fell down the stairs in May."

I commented, "When you and I talked earlier, you were positive she had fallen down the stairs on her own."

He retorted, "That was then. Now I've changed my mind about that. It could not have been a coincidence that she first had an accident on the stairs and now got murdered. That incident in May must have been the first attempt to kill her."

I commented, "Yes. I understand your reasoning."

He continued, "When Mom said that she had lost her footing and fell, she must have wanted to protect someone."

"That thought has occurred to me."

At that point of our conversation, we had arrived. There were little groups of people gathered in front of the church, all headed towards the entrance. A few faces looked familiar. I had probably seen some of these people at the art exhibit.

Guido said, "You go ahead. Per Aunt Lillian's instructions, I'm supposed to wait for the family."

The little church was already three-fourths full as I entered. I found a seat near the center. Glancing towards the altar, I caught my breath. Michael's painting depicting Millie up on the lookout was displayed on a little podium. He had captured that ageless quality about Millie to perfection. As I surveyed the figure standing by the railing, a half smile on her lips and a faraway look in her eyes, I felt a lump in my throat.

The church was filled to capacity by the time the family members walked up the center aisle and took their seats in the front pew. The tremendous strain each one of them was under showed clearly in their faces.

The pastor started by saying a few consoling words. Some of Millie's friends took turns on the pulpit describing her generosity and zest for life. Mr. Clementine hobbled to the front on his cane to face the congregation. He praised Millie's artistic accomplishments, as well as her ability to discover new talent.

The service was just coming to an end when the door was flung open and a flamboyant man in his fifties rapidly strode along the center aisle to the front of the church. I heard whispering and surprised exclamations from the people gathered around me.

As he faced the congregation, I realized we were looking at Rico Ramono.

He said, "Sorry I'm late. My flight was delayed."

Then he turned and faced Millie's portrait, bowed in front of it, and stated, "This is for you, *Cara Mia.*" And he sang Schubert's *Ave Maria* to her.

His strong and beautiful tenor voice filled the house of worship with sadness and triumph.

After coming back from the memorial luncheon, I made a reservation on the Catalina Express and reserved a rental car in Long Beach for the following day. It was time to pay the mainland a short visit. I assumed Detective Barker had crossed me off the suspect list, so his command of remaining on the island no longer applied.

Peter phoned me in the evening and I shared the events of the day.

Then he commented, "What a nice gesture of Rico Ramono to fly over from Italy to attend the service!"

I said, "It wasn't just a gesture. I think he really loved Millie and wanted to say good-bye." And I continued, "I was very impressed with him. I don't mean his singing. I've heard him sing before and his voice is superb, of course. I mean I admired the way he conducted himself as a person today. He was able to dodge the media when coming out of the church, but later, when we were gathering to enter the restaurant for the luncheon, a reporter cornered him."

Peter interrupted, "I can imagine this was bliss for the media. A murdered artist and a celebrated opera singer in one package, so to speak!"

"Yes," I said, "and a famous art critique. Mr. Carl Clementine, whom I met a week ago at Michael's art exhibit, showed up as well.

"Anyhow, coming back to Rico Ramono, I was about three yards away from him in front of the restaurant when this reporter shoved a microphone at him, asking about his former marriage and divorce from Mildred Faracelli. Rico Ramono said loud and clear, 'Mildred Faracelli met with a tragic death three days ago. We are here to honor her memory and give our last farewell. How dare you make a farce out of her life story?' Then he brushed him aside and briskly made his way to the memorial luncheon."

Peter asked, "How are you doing, Regula?"

"You mean personally or with the detecting?"

"Both."

"Well, I have not been able to cry yet. It would be a relief if I could. As far as the sleuthing goes, I have an idea, but I might be wrong. One good thing: I seem to be cleared of suspicion, as far as the police are concerned. Detective Barker's attitude towards me has changed somewhat."

He commented, "That is some progress, at least."

Then I asked, "How are you managing?"

"A little domestic mishap aside, I'm doing fine."

"What happened?"

"Oh, nothing tragic. I just messed up the laundry."

"I presume you forgot to separate the whites from the coloreds?"

"Yes. I am sporting pink boxer shorts now."

"I hope they turned a bright fuchsia pink," I retorted, and we hung up.

I lay awake that night, mulling over everything I had learned since joining the household. Rumors were a funny thing, I thought. I tried to remember what each person had told me regarding how he or she first learned about the possible push down the stairs. No one had been precise, not even Lillie.

Just before sleep overtook me, I had decided to have another talk with Jesse.

Chapter 42

◇◇◇◇◇◇◇◇◇◇◇◇◇◇◇◇◇◇◇◇

Ascending the stairs after breakfast on Sunday, I heard loud music coming from Jesse's room. It reminded me of the teenage years of my own children. Experience had taught me that music was the adolescent way of dealing with life's frustrations and pain. Getting no response to my knocking at his door, I opened it a fraction and stuck my head in.

Jesse was seated at the edge of the unmade bed, staring into space. He suddenly noticed me and turned the volume down.

I said, "I'm sorry to bother you, but I'd like to talk to you before I leave for the mainland. May I come in?"

"Sure," he said and turned the CD off altogether.

I entered, closed the door behind me and sat down on his desk chair, turning it to face him.

He said, "I thought you were going to stay and find out who murdered Mom."

I replied, "Of course I am. I'm not leaving the island for good. This is just a short visit. I'll be back by this evening."

"Oh."

Then I commented, "So you are getting your scuba diving certification tomorrow?"

"Yes." And he asked, "Do you think I'm selfish to go ahead with the dive anyhow?"

"Not at all, Jesse. Your mom would have wanted it that way."

"I think so." And repressing tears, he added, "She was going to give me a party afterwards."

I stated, "I am planning to watch when you come up from your dive and applaud when you get your certification. What time will that be, approximately?"

He said, "Around 10:30 or so."

"I'll be there!" Then I said, "Now, Jesse, I want you to try to remember something. When we talked about the fall down the stairs, you said that Aunt Lillian might have suggested your mom had been pushed. So was that the first time you heard about such a possibility?"

He replied, "I don't remember."

I continued, "Did you attempt to blackmail people at your winter residence or here on the island?"

"That I do know. It was here. Actually, it was when Aunt Lillian was visiting. She questioned us about it, and I got the idea to have some fun with everyone." He looked at me guiltily, and added, "Now I know that was stupid and wrong of me."

There was a long pause, and then I said, "Yes. I see."

I looked at my watch and then stated, "I had better get ready to catch the boat. Try to remember from whom you first learned about the push on the stairs. It is very important."

When I arrived in Long Beach, the car was ready for me. I asked the clerk behind the rental-car counter for directions to my destination. He did not know the area but let me copy the information out of a Thomas Guide.

Driving through Long Beach, I spotted a church. I stopped, parked the car and went inside.

There was a Mass in progress and I took a seat near the back. While the congregation was reciting the creed, I suddenly broke down and had myself a good cry.

The woman in the pew behind tapped me on the shoulder, whispering, "Are you all right?"

I turned around and said, "Yes. I just needed to let go."

She nodded understandingly and went back to concentrating on her Mass.

Leaving the church behind three quarters of an hour later, I felt better than I had in the last four days.

Chapter 43

◇◇◇◇◇◇◇◇◇◇◇◇◇◇◇◇◇◇◇◇

Following the directions copied from the Thomas Guide, the address Lillie had given me was relatively easy to find. The small house was located halfway down a residential block of single-family homes. I judged the neighborhood to be modest and respectable. I parked the car and walked along the path of a well-kept front yard leading to the door and rang the bell.

The woman that answered was in her seventies. She looked familiar, although I was sure we had never met.

I said, "Mrs. Albertis?"

"Yes?"

"My name is Regula Huber. I was a friend of Mildred Faracelli. I happened to be in this neighborhood and decided to stop by."

She looked at me uncomprehendingly at first, and then she said, "Oh. Mrs. Faracelli, the lady who is sponsoring Michael's paintings. Come on in."

I followed her into the living room, and she motioned me to have a seat on the sofa. She offered me something to drink, which I declined.

Then she said, "Did you say Mrs. Faracelli *was* your friend? Did you have a falling out with her?"

I replied, "Mildred Faracelli died last Wednesday."

She said, "I am sorry. Michael did not tell me she was ill."

"She was murdered," I said.

"How horrible!" Then she added, "I wonder if Michael has heard of this terrible news."

I said, "Do you see your son often?"

She replied, "No, but he calls me fairly often." Then she added, "Come to think of it, he has not called lately. It's been at least three weeks."

Then I asked, "When did you see him last?"

"In April or May. I ran into him by chance. I went to Shoreline Village for a little outing, and there he was, having lunch with a girlfriend."

"With Mildred Faracelli?"

She seemed shocked, and said, "Oh no. Mrs. Faracelli took an interest in Michael as an artist and helped open doors for him, but I'm sure there was no intimacy going on between them. We have not met, but I understand she was an older, very refined lady."

I asked, "Do you know Michael's girlfriend?"

She replied, "He introduced us, but I can't remember her name. It does not matter. When I asked about her next time he called, they had broken up."

Then I said, "I have seen your son's paintings, and I am impressed. He is very talented."

She said, "I guess he is. I like some of his work, but not all."

"Oh?"

"I don't care for nudes much. I don't like the idea of these women posing for him naked."

I said, "Oh, Mrs. Albertis, models are used to that. It is just a job to them, and they take the posing in their stride."

"Maybe, but I doubt Michael takes it in his stride. He is very easily influenced by women."

I changed the subject and said, "I like his portraits best. I think Michael has a special talent in capturing facial expressions."

She stated, "That is true, but you should not be allowed to look into someone's soul. Certain things should be kept private."

"Are you thinking of any painting in particular?"

She nodded and said, "He made a portrait of me, right after my husband died. I had no idea he was painting me at the time. When he showed it to me, I was very upset and wanted to burn it. Michael seemed shocked, saying, 'You can't ever destroy a piece of art.' He promised me that he would never show it to the public, nor try to sell it."

I thought to myself, the painting at the exhibit, titled *Grief-Stricken*! Of course! Now I know why she looks familiar.

Aloud I said, "How long have you been a widow, Mrs. Albertis?"

"Twelve years."

"Does it get easier with time passing?"

"Yes. The pain goes away, but the longing remains," she said.

"I can well understand that."

Then she asked, "Have they captured the person who murdered your friend?"

I replied, "There is an investigation under way. It was an inside job."

She shook her head and said, "That makes it even sadder."

After a pause, she added, "It will be a big shock to Michael. When he called me last time, he had just moved to Catalina Island, so he probably has not heard about Mrs. Faracelli's tragic death."

I asked, "What was his reason for moving to Catalina?"

She replied, "According to him, it was done on an artist's whim. He told me the scenery on the island is a painter's paradise."

"Yes. I can imagine that," I said.

I took my leave from Mrs. Albertis. As I drove away, I could picture the lady saying to herself, now, what exactly was that visit all about?

On the boat trip back to Avalon, I reflected on what I had discussed with Mrs. Albertis. Obviously, Michael had kept his relationship with Millie a secret from his mother. The lady thought that Mildred Faracelli was just his art sponsor. She also did not seem to know that Millie actually lived in Avalon. I presumed that after Michael had moved in with Millie, he called his mother, informing her of his relocation to the island. Mrs. Albertis was under the impression that he lived there by himself. Michael's mother struck me as being old fashioned and very proper, so I could understand that he did not want her to know about his relationship with Millie.

Mrs. Albertis ran into her son and a girlfriend in April or May. I found the timing interesting. Obviously he was already dating Millie at that time. He either broke up with the girlfriend when things got serious with Millie, or he might have kept her on the side.

The reason for not inviting his mother to the art exhibit was of course the painting, *Grief-Stricken.* I have a feeling that Pamela Norris talked him into displaying it. He had promised his mom not to show it in public. It was also clear why he had not told his mother of the murder. He did not want her to know that he lived under the same roof with Millie.

So what I had learned on this trip to the mainland was:

1. Michael might have been cheating on Millie.
2. I discovered that Mrs. Albertis did not read the *Los Angeles Times.*
3. I had solved the mystery surrounding the mother-son relationship.

Unfortunately, none of this brought me any closer to solving the mystery of Millie's murder.

Chapter 44

◇◇◇◇◇◇◇◇◇◇◇◇◇◇◇◇◇◇◇◇

Monday morning I left the house a few minutes before ten o'clock. I wanted to make sure I was on time to see Jesse come up from his dive. I parked the golf cart on the back side of the Casino and walked the short distance towards the ocean. I waited on top of the stairs leading down to the Casino Point Marine Park. I was at least 20 minutes early, so when I saw movement in the water below, it took me by surprise.

Two figures came up, and coming closer, I noticed that one of them pulled and supported the other. The person, half pulling, half carrying the other, made his way to the bottom step, and I knew there was something terribly wrong. He yelled, "Help," pulled the other person's hood off, and started to give mouth-to-mouth resuscitation.

As the hood came off, I saw that the seemingly lifeless person was Jesse. With a pounding heart, I reached for my cell phone and dialed 911.

I watched helplessly as the dive instructor kept doing mouth-to-mouth resuscitation until the paramedics arrived and took over. The reviving efforts were unsuccessful.

A couple of minutes later, Avalon's senior deputy sheriff came on the scene, and I said to him, "It's Jesse."

A small crowd had gathered, and the lieutenant made everyone move aside while the paramedics wheeled Jesse towards the ambulance vehicle.

Then he turned to me and said, "I understand you made the call to 911. Why are you here, by the way?"

I explained the reason for my being at the Casino Point Marine Park that particular morning, and then my knees gave in.

He led me to a stone bench attached to the Casino building and said, "Here. Sit down, Mrs. Huber. We can fill out the report later."

Jesse's dive instructor sat at the other end of the bench, taking off his equipment. The young man was clearly shaken.

The lieutenant sat down next to him and took the man's personal information: name, address, telephone number, et cetera.

Then he said, "Tell me what happened down there."

The instructor stated, "Jesse was on his last training dive, and we were at 60 feet. I was leading, going through kelp. Jesse was right behind me, I thought. Turning my head to point something out to him, I became aware he had been lagging behind a few yards. He was just floating; the regulator was out of his mouth. I came close to him, tried to get his attention, and then realized that he was unconscious. Trying to get him to take the regulator was unsuccessful. I brought him up as fast as was safe. I did not even make the customary safety stop of three minutes at 15 to 20 feet. Once on the surface, I gave him mouth-to-mouth, but it was useless."

The deputy sheriff asked, "What do you mean by 'as fast as was safe?'"

He replied, "No faster than one foot per second."

"What is a safety stop?"

"Normally, we hang around at 15 to 20 feet or so for about three minutes, in order to get rid of excess nitrogen. It's a precaution, so we are not likely to get the bends. But as I said, since this was obviously an emergency, I did not bother with the safety stop and took Jesse straight up."

The lieutenant said, "One foot per second; so at 60 feet without stopping, it took you one minute to get to the surface. Correct?"

"Yes, approximately," the instructor replied.

"At what time did you start your dive?"

"At 9:30."

"Do you know what time it was when you first noticed Jesse had a problem?"

The young man thought about this and then replied, "I had checked my instruments at 30 minutes into our dive. Just a few minutes afterwards, I noticed Jesse was in trouble. So I would say it was approximately 10:05."

The lieutenant asked, "Do you have any opinion of what actually happened?"

"No. I can't explain it. The only thing I can think of is that Jesse must have passed out under water - maybe a heart attack, stroke, or a seizure. I don't know. He seemed perfectly fine earlier in the dive."

"Do you know of any medical problems the boy had?"

The instructor replied, "As far as I know, Jesse was in perfect health. Before I started to instruct him, a doctor filled out and signed the necessary medical form, which stated that he was in excellent shape."

"Is it possible that Jesse for some reason panicked down there?"

"Absolutely not. He was a natural under water," the young man stated.

The senior deputy said, "I think that is all for the moment, thank you."

The instructor sadly went to his golf cart, loaded his equipment, and then drove away.

I had myself under control by that point and said, "I fear this was not an accident."

The lieutenant commented, "Too much of a coincidence. I agree with you."

He added, "After the coroner has performed an autopsy, we'll know."

Chapter 45

◇◇◇◇◇◇◇◇◇◇◇◇◇◇◇◇◇◇◇

I found Lillie in the living room. She had stacks of mail in front of her, presumably condolences. At first she did not seem to notice I was in the room. Then she looked up at me, her reading glasses on the tip of her nose.

She said, "You look like a ghost, Reg. Are you OK?"

I replied, "No, I'm not," and I proceeded to tell her the sad news.

She exclaimed, "Oh no! That's awful!" Then she asked, "Do you know what happened?"

"There will be an autopsy, and then we'll know," I said.

"Oh Reg, you don't think he was murdered too?"

"I'm afraid we have to prepare ourselves for that possibility."

We were silent for a while, and then Lillie burst out, "What is going on in this house? First Millie, and now Jesse. He was only 17, for crying out loud!"

I stated, "I came here to investigate what is going on, and instead of succeeding, two murders happened right under my nose. I should have been able to protect at least Jesse."

Lillie said, "You couldn't have known he was going to be killed."

"No, but somehow I should have," I replied.

Then she asked, "Have you told anyone yet?"

I replied, "I came across Beatrix in the hall and told her. I have not talked to anyone else."

At lunchtime, we broke the sad news to the family. Everyone was shocked and horrified.

Later, Lillie and I were alone out on the veranda, and she stated, "Millie has not even been cremated yet, and I have to think about making plans for Jesse."

Beatrix came through the sliding-glass door at that moment and said, "Excuse me for interrupting, Mrs. Robertson. What shall I tell Bruce Dillon? He is here for the two o'clock lesson. He does not know about Jesse's accident, of course."

"Send him out here. He needs to be told," Lillie said.

Informed about the latest tragedy, the tutor just stared at us, appearing unable to comprehend her words.

Then he swallowed a couple of times and finally said, "I am devastated. How horrible!"

Lillie said, "We are all in shock."

Mr. Dillon commented, "Jesse was doing really well with his schoolwork, and then he had to deal with his mom's tragic death. Now he's gone himself. I can't believe it."

Lillie said, more to herself, it seemed, "I can't think what kind of arrangements to make for him."

The young man said, "I know Jesse's wishes in that respect."

Perplexed, she asked, "You do?"

"Yes. When we had a lesson the day after his mom's death, we did not get any scholastic work done. I felt it was more important to let Jesse air his emotions instead. We talked about how he felt about all sorts of issues, and we discussed the fact that his mother's ashes will be buried up at the lookout. Jesse volunteered that in the event of his passing he would like his ashes to be scattered in the ocean. To be precise, he would like them to be dispersed at the Casino Point Marine Park."

With a lump in my throat, I said, "Yes, I can understand this would be Jesse's wish."

In the late afternoon, Detective Barker and the lieutenant arrived. The detective had us all assemble in the dining room once more.

He stated, "I am very sorry about this latest tragedy. We have reason to believe that Jesse's drowning was not accidental. Another murder is indicated. We have to question everyone again. So please make yourselves available."

Then he turned to Lillie and said, "I meant to call you, but since we are looking into Jesse's death now, I figured I might as well tell you in person. Mrs. Faracelli's body has been released. You can go ahead with the cremation."

Chapter 46

◇◇◇◇◇◇◇◇◇◇◇◇◇◇◇◇◇◇◇

It was already evening by the time I was summoned to the office to face the two law officers.

Detective Barker started by saying, "I hope you can give us some valuable information, R.A. Huber. We haven't even solved the first murder and are faced with another."

I replied, "I'll try, but I'm very much in the dark myself. It would help if I knew what exactly killed Jesse. Did you get the autopsy result?"

The detective said, "I have nothing written yet, but the coroner called me and gave me a brief oral report. I don't see any reason at this point why I shouldn't share it with you."

I said, "I appreciate that."

He continued, "The findings are the following: A fatal dose of salicylic acid was found in the victim's stomach. The central nervous system was affected, causing the victim to hyperventilate and convulse, followed by losing consciousness. The actual cause of death was drowning, but the victim would have expired regardless, without immediate medical help."

I exclaimed, "Salicylic acid? Do you mean aspirin?"

"Yes. He swallowed a fatal dose of aspirin."

"That simple," I said. Then I inquired, "Do you know how soon there would be a reaction after ingesting a fatal dose of aspirin?"

He said, "You're pretty quick. That's exactly what I asked the coroner. He put it at approximately one and a half to two hours if the victim did not consume a heavy meal at the same time. Being underwater might have sped things up a little."

And he added, "There wasn't much else in the victim's stomach, by the way."

I said, "The coroner told you Jesse might have survived with immediate medical help. What does that mean?"

"I assume he meant if a medical team could have gotten to him at the first sign of symptoms and pumped his stomach, there might have been a chance of survival."

"I see. But since he was underwater at the time, there was no possibility of that."

"Exactly."

I reflected, and then I said, "The aspirins must have been put in Jesse's Gatorade."

The detective nodded, saying, "We pretty much thought along those lines too. We questioned the housekeeper, who told us that Jesse always drank Gatorade before he went scuba diving. We also interrogated everyone who sat at the breakfast table with him this morning. Nobody gave us any useful information, however."

The lieutenant said, "This might be where you can help us out, Mrs. Huber. I understand you were one of the persons at that breakfast table."

"Yes, I was there," I agreed.

Detective Barker said, "Just so we can verify everyone else's statement, tell us what time you had breakfast, who else was there, what you noticed, et cetera."

I complied, "It was approximately 8:10 when I walked into the dining room. Guido was already seated at the table. Jesse joined us about five minutes later. There was fruit, toast, rolls, butter and jelly, coffee and a pitcher of orange juice, as well as place settings on the table.

"Beatrix appeared and sat a 20-ounce bottle of Gatorade and a glass in front of Jesse. He poured some of the drink into the glass, drank from it and ate some fruit. I offered him the breadbasket, but he declined and explained that before a dive he just ate fruit and drank a lot of Gatorade for energy, since he did not like to dive with a full stomach.

"Tony and Lisa came down maybe five minutes later. The conversation was kept at a minimum, which was understandable, given the circumstances. Jesse was the first to leave, saying he had better get ready for his scuba lesson. He took the bottle of Gatorade with him, which looked to be three fourths empty. I did not look at my watch, but I would guess it was around 8:30 at the time. I saw my friend, Lillian Robertson, out on the veranda, writing what I presumed to be thank-you notes."

The detective said, "That's it? You did not see anything unusual going on? Where did you sit, by the way?"

"I sat directly opposite Jesse. If by 'unusual' you mean did I see anyone dropping a handful of aspirin into his drink, I have to say no. I am positive no one could have tampered with the Gatorade without my seeing it."

There was a pause, and then I said, "Since I've lived amongst this household, the only person that I ever saw drinking Gatorade was Jesse. You might want to make sure and ask Beatrix if anyone else occasionally drinks that beverage, but I doubt it."

The detective inquired, "What are you driving at, exactly?"

"I think the tablets might have been put into the bottle of Gatorade anytime early that morning, or maybe even the night before. The murderer would have known that Jesse would drink it before going off to dive."

The detective eyed me keenly and stated, "Yes. That's possible. We have to talk to the housekeeper about this once more."

Then he said, "Any idea why the boy was murdered in the first place?"

"I'm afraid he must have known or seen something," I said.

"He might have blackmailed the murderer."

I stated, "I am certain he did not blackmail anyone." And I informed the two gentlemen of Jesse's earlier episode of wanting to see people's reaction concerning Mildred Faracelli's fall down the stairs.

Having told the story, I added, "He promised me he would never try to blackmail anyone again. I am sure he kept his word."

Detective Barker said, "Thank you, R.A. Huber. That's all for the moment."

As I was getting up, he ordered, "Don't announce the aspirin findings to anyone just yet."

"No, sir," I said.

I called Peter that night and poured my heart out. I told him all I knew about Jesse's murder and the events of the day.

He said, "Oh Regula, I am so sorry. You really liked that boy a lot."

"Yes, I did." And I continued, "I was aware of a change in him since Millie's tragic death. There were superficial changes: He did not wear his earrings anymore, and I'm sure he was planning to let his hair grow out. But I'm not talking about these outward signs. I noticed an inner change. After the initial shock wore off, he seemed to have grown up overnight. The rebellion seemed a thing of the past, and I am positive he had made the decision to make something of himself."

Then he asked, "You're not blaming yourself for his death, I hope?"

I replied, "Somehow I am blaming myself. I still haven't figured out what Jesse knew that prompted the murderer to silence him, but I have this strange feeling that I should know."

"Are you getting close to solving the mystery about Mildred's murder?"

"I'm getting there."

"Why not tell the police what you know?"

"It would be useless; I have no proof."

Peter said, "Please be careful, Regula!" Then he added, "Promise me you'll keep your protection handy, from now on!"

After a pause, I replied, "OK. I promise."

As soon as we ended the call, I got my pistol out of hiding and placed it in the nightstand. I felt I was keeping my promise to Peter somewhat; after all, the gun was handier kept in the nightstand than it had been inside two pieces of luggage. I knew this was a compromise and not at all what Peter had in mind. Being a lady detective certainly had its disadvantage when it came to carrying a gun. Unless you carried it openly in a holster on a belt, there weren't too many places you could hide it on your body without showing a bulge.

Before falling asleep, I was thinking about how happy Jesse had seemed, telling me all about his scuba diving experiences, exactly one week previous to that day.

Chapter 47

◇◇◇◇◇◇◇◇◇◇◇◇◇◇◇◇◇◇◇

I found Gina out on the patio the following morning. The sad events of the last days had left their mark on her face. She looked haggard and had dark circles under her eyes.

I said, "You didn't get much sleep, huh?"

She shook her head and said, "I'm thinking of moving in with Charles, while I'm on the island. I would prefer to go home to my own place, but since Detective Barker won't let us off the island, that is not an option at the moment. I can't stand it in this house anymore."

I said, "Is it that everything reminds you of your mom here?"

She looked at me, surprised, and said, "Oh, no. I don't mind that. I cherish her memory. I want to get out of here because it's creepy."

"What do you mean?"

"We all look at each other with suspicion. It was bad enough after Mom was killed, but now since Jesse's drowning, it is even worse. One of us is a killer, for crying out loud!"

I said, "I can understand how you feel."

She continued, "The police are tramping in and out like they own the place. Not too long ago, we were a happy family, and now I don't think I can sit down to another gloomy dinner in this house. I'm going to call Charles right now and tell him I'm moving into his place tonight."

She abruptly got to her feet, almost knocked down her chair, and ran into the house.

Lillie joined me a few seconds later, saying, "Gina just ran past me in a furry, it seemed. What's going on now?"

I replied, "She is apparently fed up with this house and plans to move in with Charles."

"I don't blame her!" Lillie exclaimed. She sighed and stated, "I've been on the phone with Boston on and off in the last two hours. Even though the business runs pretty smoothly without me, people tend to be afraid to make major decisions without my approval. I finally told the last person who called he should use his own judgment and leave me alone."

With an attempt at a smile, she said, "It's not just Gina. I'm afraid I'm getting cranky myself!" Then she asked, "Do you suppose we can combine the two ceremonies? What do you think, Reg?"

I stared at her, uncomprehending. "Ceremonies?"

"The ashes."

I said, "Oh, sorry. I did not follow you. You jumped from Boston to ashes."

"We could combine the two. Bury Millie's ashes on the lookout, then go down to the ocean and scatter Jesse's. What do you think? Too tacky?"

I thought about it and then said, "No. I don't think it tacky, just efficient."

Lillie stated, "OK, that's settled."

Then she said, "I wonder if we should have the portrait Michael painted of her displayed for the occasion?"

I said, "That might make it too dramatic, Lillie. Don't forget, the painting portrays Millie up on the lookout. So if you display it up there during the burial of her ashes, it might give us all the chills."

"You are right, Reg." Then she added, "I would have hesitated to ask Michael for the painting anyhow. He seems to suffer so much, it would just add to his burden."

I commented, "When I saw the painting in front of the altar at the church, it gave me quite a shock. Millie looked so real!"

Then I asked, "Was displaying that painting at the memorial service your idea?"

"No. I didn't even know of its existence. Michael must have put it there."

"The day before Millie was killed, I saw Michael working on the painting. It was supposed to be a birthday present for her."

"Oh, Reg. It's all so sad." She had a hard time controlling her emotions at that point.

Beatrix came out to the veranda and announced, "The lieutenant is here. He wants to talk to Mrs. Huber alone first, then to all of us in the dining room."

Chapter 48

◇◇◇◇◇◇◇◇◇◇◇◇◇◇◇◇◇◇◇◇

When I entered the office, only Avalon's Deputy Sheriff was seated behind the desk.

I asked, "Are we waiting for Detective Barker?"

He said, "Barker did not make it to Catalina today. He is busy with another case on the mainland."

He continued, "We talked to the housekeeper again yesterday. She confirmed that Jesse was the only person in this household who drank Gatorade. She buys it by the six-pack. Yesterday morning the bottle in question was the last one in the refrigerator. There is a six- pack kept as a reserve in the pantry.

"After we could not find the empty bottle in the household trash, we remembered that you mentioned Jesse had walked away with the almost-empty bottle of Gatorade. We figured he must have either finished drinking it on his way down or when arriving at the dive site. So last night we organized a search at the Casino Point Marine Park and found it in a trash bin there. We were informed by the lab people this morning that traces of salicylic acid -- in other words, aspirin -- were found in that bottle of Gatorade."

I asked, "I wonder if the Gatorade bottles had safety seals on them. Most bottles and containers sold nowadays come with these protective closures so no one can tamper with them before they're sold."

"Barker thought of that and asked Beatrix. Since she buys them in six-packs, the safety closures do not apply. All six bottles are packed into a single cellophane wrapping."

"I see. So anyone can unscrew the cap and put it back on again."

"Exactly," the lieutenant stated. And he added, "Anyone in the household could have added the aspirin to the bottle of Gatorade and replaced it in the refrigerator."

I said, "That seems to rule out any outsiders."

He said, "According to the housekeeper, no visitors came to the house since Mrs. Faracelli was killed, as far as she knows, not even on Saturday, the day of the memorial service. The event was held in town, so there was no reason for any outsiders to come to the residence."

I commented, "Beatrix would know. She runs this house, and I doubt any stranger would have access to it without her knowledge." After a pause, I said, "This murderer is very clever. Most people have aspirin in their possession."

The lieutenant nodded, saying, "When we first searched the rooms after Mrs. Faracelli's murder, there was aspirin in most bathrooms and people's belongings in this house, yours included, Mrs. Huber. You could open a pharmacy with the amount of aspirin kept here. At the time of the search, we were not looking for aspirin in particular; so, of course, we did not keep track of how much was in each container."

He shook his head and said, "These murders are simple, one would think. The murderer uses a tool that is conveniently lying around to stab the first victim. He kills the second with a fatal dose of aspirin, which is as easily obtained as drinking water. So we know exactly how both these murders are committed, but I'll be darned if we can ever figure out by whom."

Then he said, "We're done here for the day. I'll talk to the family in a minute. Detective Barker and I will be back, either tomorrow or the next day. In the meantime, please keep your eyes and ears open. Maybe the murderer will make a slip."

Our meetings in the dining room were becoming routine, it seemed.

The lieutenant stated, "Detective Barker and I feel you all have a right to know our findings. There is no doubt: Jesse was murdered, I am sorry to say. A fatal dose of aspirin was added to his Gatorade drink. He lost consciousness during his dive and consequently drowned. I am asking you all to please stay on the island until further notice. However, if any of you need to leave on urgent business, Detective Barker wants that person to check in with him on the mainland. I am leaving his card with you. We will be back tomorrow, or Thursday at the latest, to continue the investigation here. Let me assure you, just because we'll be absent from the household does not mean we stop working on the case. We are working on the two murder investigations around the clock."

He thanked us for our cooperation and left.

Chapter 49

◇◇◇◇◇◇◇◇◇◇◇◇◇◇◇◇◇◇◇◇

I fixed myself a sandwich for lunch and ate in solitude, out on the veranda. No one of the entire household seemed to be around. I presumed people were avoiding one another at this point. Afterwards, I strolled around on the grounds, ending up at the lookout.

As I stood at the edge of the overhang, placing my hands on the railing and surveying the harbor of Avalon below, I felt Millie's presence very strongly.

I said to myself: My dear Millie, what did you get yourself into? I wish I had figured it out in time to save you!

I was so deep in thought, I did not hear Julia's approach.

She said, "Hi. I saw you from the treehouse."

"Oh! Hi, Julia."

"I hope I'm not intruding. I know this was Mrs. Faracelli's favorite spot. So you are probably saying good-bye to her."

Again, I was amazed at this child's unusual perception.

I said, "You are right, but you are not intruding."

Then I looked at her searchingly and asked, "Do you know about Jesse?"

She replied, "Yes. The police questioned me again yesterday."

"Are you all right?"

"I cried a lot, but I'm OK now."

I nodded and then I asked, "Were you able to help Detective Barker?"

Julia replied, "No. Jesse didn't tell me anything." And she added, "The detective kept asking me to try to remember what Jesse and I talked about after his mom's death. I told him more than once that Jesse did not want to talk about his mom's murder. I was already upset after the lieutenant informed me that Jesse had been in a diving accident, so when the other policeman kept probing, Dad got mad and told him to leave me alone."

"I see."

Then she asked, "It wasn't really an accident, was it?"

"No. Jesse was murdered," I replied.

"I thought so. I mean, if it had been an accident, the police wouldn't have come to question me." She continued, "I understand the police were only doing their job, and I want them to find out who killed Jesse, but it was all very upsetting."

After a pause, I said, "I know this is painful for you, Julia, but I need to ask you a few questions concerning Jesse."

"I don't mind. I know you liked him," she said.

"When did you see Jesse last?"

"Let me see. It was last Friday."

"You did not see him Sunday, the day before he died?"

"No. Dad and I went over to the mainland on Sunday."

"I see."

Then she said, "Jesse was in the treehouse, though, on Sunday."

"How do you know?"

"He left me a note. The note said, 'Can't play after diving. Let's make it after my tutoring. See you tomorrow at about 4:30.' "

Her eyes were moist, and she added, "Then the police came over, instead."

I felt sorry for the girl and hated to pester her more.

Nonetheless, I continued, "So Jesse stayed at the treehouse by himself sometimes?"

"Oh, yes. He liked to think things out up there."

We were still standing at the edge of the lookout by the railing, when I said, "Think hard, Julia. Can you remember anything Jesse shared that had been on his mind the last few days of his life?"

She shook her head and said, "I can't think of anything."

Then she commented, "Maybe he wrote something in his journal."

I exclaimed, "He actually kept a journal? You mean like a diary?"

"Yes."

At that moment we heard a noise coming from the undercut of the ledge. I presumed someone was standing on the walkway directly below us.

I placed my index finger on my lips and led Julia away from the edge. She understood and nodded.

We walked to the farthest spot away from the edge, and I whispered, "Do you know where Jesse kept his journal?"

"Yes. It's in the treehouse," she whispered back.

Still in the same low voice, I said, "We're going back to the edge. Just let me do the talking."

She nodded.

As we walked back to the rim, I said loud and clear, "That's settled, then. Let's go ask your dad if he'll allow you to come to Avalon with me."

She said, "OK."

We walked away from the lookout in the direction of the Jacobs residence.

As soon as we were out of earshot, I said, "Don't look back."

Julia said, "Somebody was eavesdropping on us. Do you think it was the murderer?"

I answered, "Probably not, but I didn't want to take any chances."

"Do you really want me to come down to Avalon with you?"

"No. I said that for the benefit of the person that was listening. I wanted to establish a reason for heading towards your house."

Julia said, "I see. You want to go in the treehouse."

"Exactly."

As we approached the hedge that separated the two estates, she looked me up and down and then commented, "You can probably squeeze through."

I made it through the little clearing in the hedge with just a few scratches on my arms. The treehouse was a sturdy wooden structure with circular steps leading up to the top. Once on the platform that was obviously the "house" part, I was amazed at how roomy the place was. Built-in wooden benches jutted out from all four walls. A card-table was set up in the center, and I noticed numerous board games stacked on a built-in corner shelf. The place sported three windows, or rather open window frames: one facing the ocean, the second looking onto the Jacobs house and the third towards the Faracelli property.

I commented, "This is a luxury treehouse. I didn't expect it to be so sophisticated! Did your father build it for you?"

She said, "Oh, no. The treehouse was already here when Dad moved in. Apparently there was a family with lots of kids living here before."

I said, "OK, Julia, let's get down to business. Where is Jesse's journal?"

She reached over to the far-end bench, opened the lid, took out the diary and handed it to me. I was amazed. That last bench was actually a storage chest.

Before opening the journal, I asked, "Do you know when he started writing a journal?"

"A long time ago, I guess. When I first met him three summers ago, he was already writing in it."

Looking at the diary, I said, "It doesn't have a lock. Did you read it?"

"No," she replied.

"Not even since yesterday?"

"We never talked about it, but I'm sure Jesse kept the journal here because he wanted privacy. I would imagine he wrote his private thoughts down. He knew he could trust me. His death does not change that."

I looked into her eyes, saying, "You are a true friend!" Then I stated, "Can you understand that I have to take a look at it now?"

"Yes," she agreed.

I opened the journal and leafed through the last few pages. There was an entry on July 24th and another on July 27th. I read through the first one, written the day after Millie's murder.

I fought tears while reading it. Then I read the last entry, written on Sunday, the day before Jesse was killed.

I exclaimed, "Oh, Jesse, I am so sorry!"

Julia looked at me searchingly and then said, "He wrote something revealing in the journal, didn't he?"

"Yes, he did. It doesn't prove much, but it confirms my theory," I said.

Then I ordered, "Julia, I want you to go into your house and stay there for the rest of the day. If someone comes to your door, let your dad answer it."

She looked at me, dumbfounded, saying, "But I'm not in any danger. I don't know anything."

"The murderer does not know that."

She agreed, "OK. I'll go home. What are you going to do?"

I said, "I am going down to Avalon and pay the Sheriff Station a visit. I'll tell the lieutenant what I suspect."

And pointing to the journal in my hand, I said, "This isn't exactly evidence, but I want to show it to him. I'll only let him read the very last entry."

She nodded, and we descended the steps and left the treehouse behind.

Chapter 50

◇◇◇◇◇◇◇◇◇◇◇◇◇◇◇◇◇◇◇

I needed to make a quick stop at my room before heading down to Avalon. I packed wallet, cell phone, Jesse's journal, cigarettes and lighter, just in case, into my handbag.

Once in the garage, I noticed only the yellow golf cart was missing. I hopped into the red one and was on my way.

As I was coming around the first curve in the road, a golf cart with a yellow suntop came into view, climbing up from the opposite direction. Beatrix was obviously on her way home. When even with each other, we waved.

Before the next bend, I decided I'd better slow down a bit and pressed on the brakes. I felt no reaction whatsoever. I braked again, without result.

I said to myself, aloud, "Oh my God! No brakes!"

I instinctively reached for the hand brake and touched only air. Of course, there is no hand brake on a golf cart.

I talked to myself again, "Don't panic, Regula! Think!"

My first thought was to jump out, but I had gathered a lot of speed by that time. I remembered a steep driveway leading up to a house on the north side of the road.

Coming around the next curve, I yelled, "Hold on tight to the steering wheel, old girl! Don't lose control!"

Where the heck was that driveway, I thought, while I felt my heart pounding.

There! I suddenly spotted the driveway. I jerked the steering wheel and went up and over the ramp. Protecting my face with one arm, I headed straight into a big bush, where the cart came to a halt.

Collecting myself and making my way out of the thicket, I exclaimed, "This was too much of an adrenalin rush, even for me!"

I checked myself over. On one side of my head, an "egg" started to develop where I had bumped against the suntop support strut of the cart. I also noticed a few scratches on my arms and legs, caused by landing in the bush. Other than that, I was as good as new.

First I decided I had earned a smoke, and then I walked up to the house on which driveway I was stranded. I rang the doorbell, but apparently there was no one home. I always keep a pen and note paper in my purse, so I wrote a note: "Please do not remove cart until police have checked it out. Thank you!" I attached the note to the red suntop and started to walk up the hill towards the Faracelli residence.

On my hike up, I called Lillie. I was glad I had programmed her cell phone number into my phone.

I said, "I had a little accident. I'll explain later. Here is what I want you to do" - -

Lillie interrupted, "What accident? Where are you, Reg?"

"Someone tampered with my golf cart brakes. I am a little ways down the road and on my way back up to the house."

"Are you OK?"

"Yes. I have a few cuts and bruises, but I'm fine." Then I said, "Now listen, Lillie. First of all, where are you in the house, and where is everyone else?"

She replied, "I just came up to my room. I heard some banging in the kitchen before I came up, so I assume Beatrix is back from shopping and is putting groceries away. I think Gina is in her room packing. I don't know where everyone else is."

I asked, "Is anyone on the veranda?"

"I don't think so."

"OK. Lillie, stay in your room. Give me about ten minutes, then call the Sheriff Station. Tell the lieutenant someone sabotaged my cart and it can be found stuck in a bush, next to the driveway of the house situated at the north side of the road, about a quarter of a mile down from the Faracelli house. Ask the lieutenant to come to the Faracelli residence as soon as possible. I have information for him. See you soon," and I hung up.

Chapter 51

◇◇◇◇◇◇◇◇◇◇◇◇◇◇◇◇◇◇◇◇

I did not see or hear anyone on my way to the back of the house. I let myself in through the veranda. The sliding-glass door was open, as usual. I quickly went upstairs and into my room, unobserved. I placed Jesse's journal in the old hiding place in back of the walk-in closet, took my pistol out of the nightstand, rummaged through my undies for ammunition, loaded the piece, and was out the door.

Descending the stairs, then pausing in the hallway, I heard murmurs coming from the kitchen. Getting closer, I noticed the kitchen door was just a crack open, so I could hear the voices clearly at that point. I stood by the door and listened. I thought to myself, this is easier than I expected: I have them both together.

I heard Beatrix's voice, "That was very stupid of you! Haven't I taught you, if planning a murder, you make sure there is no doubt about the outcome? When I passed the Huber woman on my way up, she was going fast, but it did not look to me like she was out of control. She probably crashed further down and might only have gotten injured, not killed."

Then she said, "Now tell me exactly what you overheard beneath the lookout."

What I took for Michael's voice answered, "The girl said that Jesse kept a journal. Then they moved farther away and I couldn't hear them anymore. A few moments later, they came back within earshot, and Mrs. Huber said they were going to ask Julia's father for permission to let the girl go down to Avalon with Huber."

Beatrix stated, "The kid was not with Huber when I saw her. Besides, we don't know if the girl knows anything.

We also don't know whether or not there is anything incriminating in that journal. What the devil were you thinking anyhow, Michael?"

He said, "I first went to Jesse's room and searched for the journal. When I couldn't find it, I guess I panicked. I thought Mrs. Huber and Julia knew something and were planning to go down to Avalon to talk to the lieutenant. I wanted to stop them, and" - -

She interrupted, "You already told me what you did. Don't tell me again!"

Then she said, "Why didn't you wait until I was back, and let me make the decisions?"

"I told you, I panicked. I figured there was no time to lose."

I heard Beatrix say, "OK. What's done is done. There isn't much time, but I'll patch it up." She continued, "Now tell me, did you at least wear gloves when you searched Jesse's room and when you cut the cable?"

"Yes, I did," he answered.

After a pause, I heard Beatrix's voice again, "We don't have much time. Someone probably already alerted the police, and I expect they're on their way. When the police get here, you act dumb, Michael. Shouldn't be too hard for you," she said sarcastically.

Then she said, "You leave the kid to me. She probably knows where the journal is. If she knows anything else, I'll get it out of her and then decide if she needs to be silenced. As far as the Huber woman is concerned, I'll play it by ear, depending on how badly she is injured and how much she knows. I doubt that she is actually dead."

Then I heard Beatrix say, "Get out of here now, and don't come near me in the next few days."

As the door fully opened, I stood with arms extended, in my pistol stance, and said, "Both of you, stay as you are."

Michael just stared at me.

Beatrix had recovered fast and shouted, "I knew you were trouble ever since you first came to this house!"

I calmly said, "The deputy sheriff is on his way up. In the meantime, I'll see to it that neither one of you makes a move."

Inwardly, I prayed: Come quickly, law enforcers, I can't hold this stance for long!

Glaring at me, Beatrix continued, "You can't prove a thing!"

I countered, "I know it all, and I also know why! Listening to your conversation with Michael just now enlightened me about today's happenings, as well."

At that moment the doorbell chimed, and I knew the lieutenant and his people had arrived.

Chapter 52

◇◇◇◇◇◇◇◇◇◇◇◇◇◇◇◇◇◇◇◇

The next day, Wednesday, I joined Lillie for lunch on the veranda.

I said, "It has been exactly two weeks since I came to Catalina. Somehow, it seems a lot longer." And I added, "I made a boat reservation. I leave at 3:30 this afternoon."

Lillie urged, "Are you sure you don't want to stay for the ashes ceremonies?"

"Yes, I'm sure," I answered. "I've already said my good-byes to Millie and Jesse. It is time for me to go home."

She nodded and said, "I can understand you want to get home to Peter."

"Yes, and Peter is getting anxious himself. He is going through a spell of writer's block, at the moment. He apparently blames it on missing my cooking, amongst other things."

Then I said, "The lieutenant called me a few minutes ago. He just gave me a brief update and said he will share it with the family later."

Lillie asked, "What did he say?"

I replied, "They examined the golf cart, and it had definitely been sabotaged. Golf carts don't have brakes in the sense that cars do. They only have rear-wheel mechanical brakes, which are connected to the brake pedal by cable. When you step on the brake pedal, it pulls this cable to stop the cart. So, on the red suntop cart, the cable had been cut in order to disable the brakes."

She commented, "That simple! And of course everyone knew that you drove the red golf cart."

I continued, "He also gave me a message from Detective Ron Barker: On interrogation, Michael had broken down and confessed to the murder of Millie, and to conspiracy to murder in Jesse's case, as well as the attempted murder on me. Beatrix, on the other hand, is holding out, denying everything."

I added, "Detective Barker wants me to be prepared to be called as a witness for the prosecution in Beatrix's trial at some time in the future."

We sat in silence, and then Lillie asked, "Why did they do it?"

I replied, "For money, of course."

She looked at me, perplexed, and said, "I don't understand. What money?"

Eyeing her carefully, I stated, "It might be a consolation to you that Millie was ill. Or did you already know?"

"No, but I was wondering why you wanted her doctor's name. What was wrong with her?"

"I suspect cancer, but I can't be sure."

Lillie said, "I don't understand. Why did she keep quiet about it?"

I replied, "Millie kept a lot of secrets. She was secretly married to Michael."

"What?" She exclaimed.

I said, "All right, Lillie. Here is how I came to some of my conclusions. Millie took a prescription medicine called Sehydrin. There was no doctor's name on the pill container, and I suspected she might have obtained the medication on the black market. I asked her what she took these pills for, and she said it was to relieve her arthritis pains. I did not believe this statement of hers. I don't want to bore you with a long story, but I looked into it and found out she was seeing an oncology and neurology specialist."

Lillie said, "That does indicate cancer."

I continued, "Guido told me that he ran into his mother and Michael unexpectedly in Las Vegas. It occurred to me that the pair might have gotten married in Vegas and kept it a secret. I have a colleague in that town, who checked this out for me, and then confirmed my hunch.

"When Millie went to see her lawyers, I wondered whether a new will was in the making. I found out from Mr. Samuelson that Millie came to sign 'wills.' By the way, this statement of Mr. Samuelson's about 'wills', in the plural, is still a puzzle to me."

She asked, "When did you first think Michael was the murderer?"

"It came to me slowly, step by step. My mind kept coming back to Millie's fall down the stairs. She obviously must have known whether she fell or was pushed. First I thought that someone pushed her and she was protecting that person by claiming she had fallen on her own. Then, after talking to everyone concerned, I changed my mind. All her stepchildren were sure no one had pushed Millie. When I asked Jesse, 'Why are you sure your mom fell,' he answered, 'She said so.' Such a simple statement, but it got me on the right track.

"The day before Millie died, I had a talk with Michael. Out of all the people in the household, he was the only one that thought it possible Millie was pushed! Mind you, very cleverly, he was not precise about this claim. He merely stated that it was possible. After thinking his statement over that night, plus all the facts I had gathered that day, I deduced the following:

Millie was sick and kept it a secret.

Millie and Michael were married and they kept their marriage a secret.

Millie had simply fallen down the stairs. Michael, the only person not present in the house at the time of her fall, wanted it to look like an attempted murder.

Millie had gone to the mainland that day to sign a new will, or wills, which she also kept secret from her family.

Millie's sculpture creation of Michael showed an

expression on his face that I took for a mixture of guilt and remorse. This, of course, was pure assumption on my part, and I might have been wrong.

All this clearly indicated that Millie knew what was going on.

"The following morning, I decided to have it out with Millie, but I was too late. I found her murdered instead."

Lillie asked, "Did you know that Beatrix was in cahoots with him?"

I replied, "Not just then. I came to that conclusion later."

"When?"

"I went to see Michael's mother the day after the memorial service. I had a feeling then that there was a woman involved, or at least that Michael had a girlfriend on the side. I did not associate Beatrix with him at that point. Beatrix is a very clever woman. She instilled the idea in everyone that she and Michael did not like each other. It was not overdone, so it was very believable.

"During a conversation I had with her early on, she cleverly made up a boyfriend, conveniently away on an African Safari. That way, she tried to plant the idea in my head that, having a boyfriend, there was no question of her being interested in Michael. As I got to know her better, I realized that telling me something about her personal life was very out of character. So actually, this boyfriend-on-Safari story worked against her.

"My suspicion of Beatrix being involved came after Jesse was killed. Who else would have had a better opportunity to spike Jesse's Gatorade with aspirin? I also figured that the murderer must have had some medical knowledge, in order to know how many aspirins would consist of a fatal dosage. During the course of a conversation, Beatrix had mentioned that she first studied to become a nurse, then changed her mind and majored in home economics.

"And then it all made sense to me. Beatrix was the

mastermind behind these crimes. She must have coached Michael as to the exact spot to insert that little sgraffito tool in order to cause instant death. Michael was weak and easily influenced by her. He obviously had a sexual attraction to Beatrix but at the same time loved Millie in his own way. I could tell there was a turmoil going on within him."

Lillie commented, "So Michael murdered Millie and Beatrix killed Jesse. Who tampered with your golf cart?"

I said, "That was Michael, and, of course, it was a big mistake from their point of view. Cutting the cable to the golf cart brakes was the only crime that was not masterminded by Beatrix. When Michael overheard my conversation with Julia, learning about a journal Jesse had kept, he thought it was crucial to find that journal. When he couldn't find it in Jesse's room, he panicked. While eavesdropping, he also heard me say that Julia and I planned to go down to Avalon together. Thinking that we both knew something that might incriminate him, he felt it was essential to stop us from seeing the lieutenant. He decided he couldn't wait for Beatrix to come back from grocery shopping to consult with her.

"Actually, he did us a favor by cutting that cable. I doubt there would have ever been enough evidence to convict those two without my overhearing their conversation in the kitchen."

She inquired, "What was in the journal that was so dangerous to him, anyhow?"

"Very little, actually. There was nothing in the diary that could be used as evidence. I didn't even show it to the lieutenant. There was no need to do so after I overheard their kitchen episode."

Then I said, "I'll get the journal. Be right back. I was planning to give it to you before I left."

Coming back from my room, I handed her Jesse's diary and said, "It's sad, but just read the last two entries."

She complied, and read aloud:

"July 24th - Yesterday Mom was murdered. I am so upset; I don't know what to do. Now I don't have anybody left who gives a damn about me. She must have been killed while I was sitting up here in the treehouse. I did not see anyone go into the studio, of course, since that big tree hides my view. It's time to go to dinner. I'm not hungry.

July 27th - I am getting my diving certification after my last lesson, tomorrow. I'm sure Mom would understand that I'm taking this lesson anyhow, even though she just died. Mrs. Huber thinks so too. Oh! I just remembered something. I think it was Michael who first told me about Mom having been pushed down the stairs. Mrs. Huber said it was important. I can't see why. I'll ask Michael. I hope he remembers exactly when it was that he told me. Then maybe I can report something helpful to Mrs. Huber."

Lillie closed the journal, and said, "Poor, dear, Jesse." Then she stated, "But it doesn't look to me like the boy knew anything incriminating at all!"

I said, "No, he didn't. I blame myself for his death. The way I figure it, he might have innocently gone to Michael and said something like, 'Remember when you told me about Mom having been pushed down the stairs? Try to think of the exact date you told me about it. Mrs. Huber thinks it's important, and I want to help her.'

"Then, I imagine Michael informed Beatrix of this, and she deduced correctly that if I found out it was Michael who started that rumor, I would figure out why and consequently solve the whole mystery. I was on the mainland that day, so she silenced Jesse the next morning before he could talk to me. That was extremely quick planning on her part."

Lillie shivered and said, "What an absolutely horrible woman! Yet, I admit, I always liked her. I know Millie thought the world of her too."

Then she said, "So Millie's accident on the stairs was just a coincidence?"

"Yes," I stated. "I noticed that Millie sometimes had a hard time controlling her right hand and leg, so a misstep and, consequently, a fall could have been very likely. I imagine Beatrix could not resist using that accident to her and Michael's advantage."

After a pause, she said, "You said they did it for money, but even if Millie was married to Michael, I am 100% sure she would never disinherit her children. Michael might have inherited a part of the fortune, but Millie would always have provided for the kids. I am absolutely positive of that."

I said, "Oh, I am sure you're right about that, but Michael might have thought that being married to Millie, without her having made a new will, would automatically make him the sole heir. Don't forget, the Faracellis, as well as Jesse, were Millie's stepchildren, not her actual flesh and blood."

"Yes. I see what you mean. And come to think of it, even a fifth of Millie's assets would still provide a small fortune." And she added, "After I contact Mr. Samuelson, we'll know the provisions made in Millie's will."

Then she sighed and said, "What a waste of Michael's talent!"

"Oh, they might let him paint murals on the prison walls," I commented.

Despite the sad occasion, I got a smile out of Lillie.

EPILOGUE

On a hot day in mid August, sitting in my office in Pasadena, grateful for the well air-conditioned room, I received a legal-size envelope in the mail. On opening it, I found a letter from the law offices of Samuelson, Rosenbaum & Blight, as well as a sealed standard-size envelope addressed to R.A. Huber, Private Detective.

I read the letter with the law office letterhead first. Dated August 12th, it read:

"Dear Mrs. Huber,

Pursuant to the sad and shocking news of Mildred Faracelli's, alias Mildred Albertis, death, I am sending you a sealed letter, which was attached to will number one, addressed to you and written by your friend. I don't know the content of the letter, but I would imagine it involves some kind of clarification.

"I feel that I owe you an explanation on my part, as well. Mildred Faracelli and Lillian Robertson were both old, established clients. Our firm had already served their father as estate lawyers, although that was before my time. I handled Mildred Faracelli's estate. It is quite a substantial estate, I might add.

"Approximately ten days before her death, Mrs. Faracelli came to me with new instructions about the disposal of her estate, after her demise. Those instructions were the following:

1. She informed me that she had recently married but wanted the marriage kept secret for the time being. Her new name was Mildred Albertis.
2. She wanted our firm to draw up two new wills with respective living trusts, each drawn up in her new name.

3. Will number one was to benefit all her stepchildren, the estate being equally divided between them.
4. Will number two was to benefit all her stepchildren, plus her husband, Michael Albertis, the estate being divided equally between all parties.
5. Will number one was to come in effect if her death was the result of unnatural causes, such as murder, suicide, or accident.
6. Will number two was to come in effect if her death was the result of natural causes, such as illness.

"These wills were, obviously, very unorthodox, and I tried to talk Mrs. Faracelli/Albertis out of making them. I pointed out to her that if she had any kind of inclination her life was in danger, going to the police was the correct course of action to take. Mrs. Faracelli insisted she knew what she was doing and was extremely decisive in her manner. (I had always considered her a vague person, until that day.)

"I reluctantly agreed to draw up the wills according to her instructions. I knew that if I refused, she would find a different law firm who would abide by her wishes.

"The day you called, Mrs. Faracelli/Albertis had come to sign the documents. She also handed me two sealed letters. The letter addressed to you was to be attached to will number one and forwarded to you after her death if will number one came into effect. The other was addressed to Michael Albertis and was to be handed to him should will number two come into effect. I know now, this took place the day before she was killed. When you phoned, your name was not unfamiliar to me. Not only had I learned it from Lillian Robertson, but I had also seen 'R.A. Huber, Private Detective' written on the envelope attached. I deduced that you attempted to help Mrs. Faracelli, hence my willingness to answer your question.

"I am now acting on behalf of Mrs. Faracelli's/Albertis's heirs, namely, Tony Faracelli, Gina Faracelli and Guido Faracelli. I have recently been informed that her stepson, Jesse Limburg, also met with a violent death.

"I remain, sincerely yours,

Steve Samuelson."

Then I opened the attached, sealed envelope and found a letter written in Millie's handwriting. It was dated July 21st, and it read:

"Dear Reg,

By the time you read this, my troubles will be over. Please don't blame yourself for anything, and don't be sad.

"I owe you an explanation. At the beginning of this year, having endured numerous testing and CAT scans, I found out I suffered from an inoperable brain tumor. The doctors expected me to live six to nine months. My options of treatment looked very bleak. I said no to chemo and radiation therapy. I found the unconventional Sehydrin medication most beneficial.

"At first, I kept my condition secret because I did not want people to feel sorry for me. Later, I guess, it was out of selfishness.

"When Michael came on the scene and I felt strongly attracted to him, I allowed myself one last 'fling.' When Michael proposed to me, I was on the verge of telling him about the brain tumor. I changed my mind, however, when he suggested that we keep our marriage a secret. He tried to convince me that I was pushed down the stairs. Yes, Reg, Michael was the one who spread that rumor. He hinted to me, one of my children had tried to kill me. I did not know it then but realized later that he wanted to establish an attempt on my life was made before he had joined the household. Now, I might be impaired by my illness, but darn it, I know I lost my footing that night in May and just simply fell.

"So I asked myself, why would Michael make up such a story? The reason he gave for keeping the marriage a secret was to protect me. He said that if the children thought we just lived together, our relationship might be temporary in their eyes. All rubbish, of course, but I played along. I knew that Michael did not want to marry me for my blue eyes! I said yes to the matrimony and yes to the secrecy. We flew to Las Vegas and got married. You can imagine what a fool I felt, eloping at my age!

"As soon as I had transferred my household to Catalina for the summer, Michael moved in. I'm sure you've noticed that Michael treats me very nicely. In a lot of ways we are happy, even to the present day. He is a gentle and wonderful lover. When you read this letter, Michael will have murdered me, unless I'm totally wrong. (I am writing him a letter of apology, just in case will number two should become effective, but I don't think I'm wrong.)

"The vague realization that Michael plans to kill me came to me after his proposal. So I said to myself, I could turn this to my advantage.

"Now, Reg, you've got to understand a few things. I don't have long to live anyhow. My condition is worsening. My right arm and leg are harder to control with every new day. Eventually I won't have the use of them at all. My headaches and loss of eyesight are rapidly getting worse, as well.

"The medication helps, but it does not halt the disease. When the day comes -- and I know I'm getting there rapidly -- that I won't be able to express myself artistically, I won't want to live any longer.

"So, my mind is made up. I'd much rather be killed quickly than become more and more useless.

"I know that the driving force behind Michael's actions and the master planer of the murder is a woman. I know Michael has been cheating on me. I have no concrete knowledge of this, but there are little signs here and there.

At first, I thought it might be Pamela Norris or maybe someone I don't know.

"Then, one day, I came back from the mainland on an earlier boat then expected. I saw Michael and Beatrix together on the beach, and it all made sense to me. It is very clever the way they pretend not to like each other. I imagine they had known one another a long time. Beatrix might have sought employment with me, with their plan in mind already, over two years ago. (That is only a guess on my part.) Remember, I had total confidence in her. Michael's meeting with me was staged. Beatrix knew that I could not possibly pass an artist's paintings without a glance!

"So I know what's coming, but of course I don't know how and when. I also know that you will figure it out, Reg, but hopefully not in time to interfere. I noticed how you looked at me when I took the Sehydrin. I could tell you didn't believe I suffered from arthritis. I also realize you were very perceptive when you looked at the bronze I made of Michael. When Michael posed for me, he was torn in his feelings. On the one hand he was really fond of me; on the other, he had already committed to do the deed. I did not know this myself at the time but became aware of the expression later.

"I am glad you are here. You amuse me!

"Feel free to show this letter to Lillie and the children, if you think they can handle it.

"There is no doubt in my mind that Lillie will take care of Jesse. The Faracelli children will be OK, I'm sure.

"I had a wonderful life. Sorry I am taking this way out.

Love, Millie."

Wiping away a tear rolling down my cheek, I said aloud:

"Tournons le farceur!"

The joke is on you, lover boy.

www.ingramcontent.com/pod-product-compliance
Lightning Source LLC
LaVergne TN
LVHW091044080826
845145LV00002B/615